a song over miskwaa rapids

Also by Linda LeGarde Grover
Published by the University of Minnesota Press

The Road Back to Sweetgrass
In the Night of Memory

a song
over
miskwaa
rapids

A Novel

Linda LeGarde Grover

University of Minnesota Press

MINNEAPOLIS

LONDON

Published by the University of Minnesota Press
111 Third Avenue South, Suite 290
Minneapolis, MN 55401-2520
http://www.upress.umn.edu

ISBN 978-1-5179-1462-2 (hc)
ISBN 978-1-5179-1482-0 (pb)

Library of Congress record available at
https://lccn.loc.gov/2023018634.

Printed in the United States of America on acid-free paper

The University of Minnesota is an equal-opportunity educator and employer.

30 29 28 27 26 25 24 23   10 9 8 7 6 5 4 3 2 1

For the mindimooyenyag,
seen and unseen we hold things together.

contents

niijiwag gaye indinawemaaganag

friends and relatives

Mindimooyenyag-iban who although unseen are still with us

Therese Gallette: mother of Half-Dime (Louis) LaForce and mother-in-law of Artense

Artense LaForce: wife of Half-Dime LaForce and daughter-in-law of Therese

Maggie LaForce: daughter of Half-Dime and Artense; first marriage to Andre Robineau; second marriage to Louis Gallette; grandmother to Margie

Grace Dionne: mother of Dale Ann Dionne Minogeezhik

Beryl Duhlebon: related to Margie and the LaForce family; lives next door to Margie

Rose (Sis) Sweet: longtime friend of Beryl

Among the living

Margie Robineau: granddaughter to the LaForce and Gallette families; lives at Sweetgrass, the LaForce allotment land, which was previously the home of the Muskrat/Washington family; partner to Zho Wash, a tribal Elder who is no longer living

Crystal Washington Bjornborg: Margie's daughter; married to Dag Bjornborg

Joey Bjornborg: Crystal's son; grandson of Margie and Dale Ann

Theresa Dooley: longtime friend of Margie; married to Michael Washington

Michael Washington: son of Zho Wash (Joseph Washington) and descendant of the Muskrat/Washington family; married to Theresa; elected representative on the Mozhay Point Tribal Council

Merrilee Washington: daughter of Theresa Dooley and Michael Washington

Dale Ann Dionne Minogeezhik: daughter of Grace Dionne; friend of Margie and Theresa; married to Mozhay Point Tribal Chair Jack Minogeezhik; mother of Dag Bjornborg, grandmother of Joey Bjornborg

Eugene Dionne: longtime friend and distant cousin of Dale Ann Dionne

Jack Minogeezhik: longtime tribal chair of the Mozhay Point Band of Ojibwe Tribal Council; married to Dale Ann Dionne

waking song

AN HOUR BEFORE DAWN one early fall day on the LaForce allotment land, the long fingers of the sun pushed at the edge of the dark sky, lightening the horizon and waking a robin who cautiously poked his head from the woodpile next to the Sweetgrass cabin. Swiveling his head to the right and to the left and back again, looking with one eye and then the other for predators—a fox, a hawk, perhaps even a lynx— he squeezed the rest of his body from the space where he had slept, thanking the Creator for Margie Robineau's son-in-law and grandson, who had piled the pieces of split log loosely enough for air to circulate. He perched, preened the long feathers of his wings, then flew suddenly skyward, set-tling on the topmost branch of the tallest aspen. From here, toes wrapped tightly around the swaying branch, he could see all of the Mozhay Point land that lay along the road from Sweetgrass. East past the Chi Waabik Casino in the Woods and the Mozhay Point tribal complex and school. To his west was the Lost Lake boat landing and a thick greenery of trees that hid the road from view, and finally, Half-Dime Hill, the Miskwaa Rapids, and the state park visitor center. Below in the cabin on the LaForce allotment lands known as Sweetgrass, Margie and her grandson, seventeen-year-old Joey Bjornborg, slept in the near-darkness of the predawn.

*

As the oblique pink light at the edge of the horizon began to widen, several mindimooyenyag-iban emerged from the woods surrounding the Sweetgrass cabin—Beryl Duhlebon and Sis Sweet from next door, where Beryl's turquoise trailer had stood when she was alive; Maggie LaForce from the frieze of red sumac leaves that lined the driveway, the sumac leaves in autumn that Maggie had loved when she was alive; and Therese LaForce and her daughter-in-law, Artense, stepping lightly over the site of the long-sodded-over outhouse, dug the deepest on the Mozhay Point reservation lands by Artense's husband, Louis, when he was alive. Each carried a lawn chair of webbed plastic woven over lightweight aluminum that they unfolded and set in a semicircle in the yard.

"Mino gizheb; it looks to be a lovely day," said Beryl, patting the four large curls at the front of her perfectly styled updo. "Gaa-pi, my dear?" she asked Sis, offering a pink-flowered ceramic mug.

"Oh, my, yes; I love Beryl's coffee, almost thick enough to stand up a spoon in," answered Sis. "Any for you ladies?"

"Thank you; we have brought niibish today." Maggie and her grandmother Therese saluted with their teacups, Maggie daintily and Therese sloshing liquid into her saucer. "Mother, Nokom, giwi minikwewin niibish, ina?"

"After we have practiced, daughter." Artense held out a palmful of small stones. "Today is the day, remember." She tossed a pebble into the air, twirled and caught it with one hand behind her back. Beryl applauded politely.

"Very fancy, but can you hit anything? Second branch up on that tamarack there. That twig right in the middle." Therese, the oldest of the women, turned to throw her pebble sideways, as if skipping a stone into Lost Lake. The pebble skimmed the twig, which shivered.

Artense sniffed, her long nose pointing toward the tallest aspen. "The leaf at the end of the branch from the top, right underneath that robin." Her eyes sighted down the length of her nose; her throw was overhead and powerful.

"Missed!" Therese danced in delight, the ribbons that bound her wool leggings around her slender ankles waving. *"Went right through the tree and didn't even faze the robin!"*

"Nabadamin, daga, ladies, minawaa minikwe gaapi dash niibish, ikwewag. Sit down and have some coffee. It's still early; there is still plenty of time to practice." Who would be the best choice for the important work to be done today, Maggie wondered. Powerful Artense or her crafty mother-in-law, Therese?

"Beautiful morning," the robin said to himself, "and time to begin. *Opiichii, opiichii niin!*"

His song, a solitary voice repeating several rounds of his wake-up song, *Opi chii, opii chii niin; opiichii, nagamo daa!* was joined by other robins who woke and joined, each flying to a branch that swayed with the bird's weight and the sweetgrass-scented breeze from the swamp side of the LaForce land. Lacing phrases and melodies of their own compositions and spirits, robins were joined by cardinals, chickadees, each chiming in with its part of the story song, some notes long and assertive, some more of a whistle, some a chatty warble.

As the song brought brightness to the edge of the sky, the back door of the Sweetgrass cabin opened, and Margie stepped out onto the porch, stretching her arms over her head. "Beautiful morning," she called back into the house. "Are you awake, Joey? My, can you hear that bunch of robins at the top of the popple?"

In the front room, her grandson sat up on the couch where he slept when he stayed at Sweetgrass, wrapped in a quilt. "I'm awake, Grandma—did you make coffee? Want me to get you a cup?"

"Eyaa, I would love a cup, migwech. Hey, aniin ikido coffee?"

"Makade mashkiki waboo."

"Migwayaak. Or . . . gaapii!" both laughed.

"I'll drink it on the front stairs," Margie said. As she listened to Joey moving around inside the house she watched the birds soar and dip over the roof of the cabin and back up to the trees, lighting on swaying branches. Turning her head from one side to the other, as the first robin of the morning had done, she unconsciously shaped her mouth into the little *o* that was her habit when she was thinking. The Creator had given the birds the gift of memory and song, and with that the obligation to be messengers and story keepers, which she had learned from Joey's grandfather and namesake, Joseph Washington. What was in the morning song?

"Opii chi, opii chi," she sang softly to herself and called into the house, "You know how Zho Wash used to say that people and birds could talk to each other long ago? That the words to the bird songs are everything that has ever happened, and that we are in the song, too?"

"My mom told me she heard that from Grandpa Zho, how people and the birds and animals all could talk with each other, but we can't anymore."

Yes, Crystal, who Zho Wash had thought would carry the stories she learned to the next generations, would have told her son. She had asked Margie the morning after he was born, when the birds sang loudly over Mozhay Point, "Do you think we will ever be able to understand what they are singing?"

Margie had addressed her daughter by the nickname given her by Zho Wash: "Who knows, Opiichii-Nagamo? Maybe sometime we'll find that out."

"Geget; that time will come, but not yet, Margie-ens. You have work to do." Maggie invisibly ruffled Margie's bangs, which stood up nearly straight, waving as blown by a morning breeze, until Margie smoothed them down.

"She will need our help, Maggie," said Therese. "That is what we are here for today, all of us. . . . Niibish, Artense? Minikwe daa."

"One more." Artense picked up a small pebble from the ground next to the stairs and pointed her nose at the red-leaved bushes that lined the driveway. "Over the sumac, all the way to the mailbox." She narrowed her eyes; her mouth formed the little o in the way of the LaForce women; twisting her body a quarter-turn to the right, she shifted her weight from her left foot to her right as she hurled. The stone, spinning, sailed the length of the sumac and disappeared, then hit the metal mailbox with a ping!

A grackle cheered with the rhythm of Beryl and Maggie's applause; Sis's whistle blended into the melody of a veery's calling out his admiration of the throw.

Therese nodded approvingly. "You will do well today, daughter."

Smiling, Artense hunched her shoulders modestly.

*

"Here's your coffee, Grandma." Joey handed Margie her cup, and the two sat on the front steps as overhead the birdsong, led by the first robin of the day, recounted in warbles, chirps, whistles, and squawks all that they had heard and remembered, passed down through more generations than birds or humans could count, over the lands of Mozhay Point.

part i.
naanoomaya, 2022

half-dime hill

AFTER WRITING AND REWORKING her statement for the upcoming Tribal Executive Council meeting, Margie Robineau decided that if she added anything else she would run over her speaking time or risk losing the attention of the council representatives: Chairman Jack Minogeezhik, Secretary–Treasurer Becky Hautala, urban communities representative Fred Simon, and Mozhay tribal neighborhoods representatives Annette Buck and Michael Washington. As she wrote she had tallied the likelihood of the councilmembers' votes on whether or not to continue with the acquisition of the LaForce allotment lands acreage if she, Margie, didn't agree to their proposal. As chair, Jack would vote only in the event of a tie. Becky would likely move to proceed, and Fred to table the motion. She could not predict Michael's or Annette's votes.

Margie thought that the tribal council would eventually win, but she was not going to make it easy for them. The evening before, she had donned her late aunt Beryl Duhlebon's lucky earrings—a pair of dangly brick-stitched butterflies Beryl had worn to Bingo, where she had won most nights. Sliding her feet into her Danskos, which Margie thought were too clunky but were the highest heels she owned, she considered wearing Beryl's lucky Mickey Mouse sequined sweater, too, as she began practicing her statement to the mirror in the bedroom of the family allotment house.

"Boozhoo, everyone. I am Margie Robineau of the LaForce and Gallette families, Mozhay Point band member, and direct descendant of Half-Dime LaForce, who was allotted the forty acres of land that we call Sweetgrass. Migwech for allowing me to speak today about your proposal to purchase the allotment.

"Like it is with many land allotments, there are dozens of descendants who have inherited shares of Sweetgrass through probate court after our ancestors died without wills. I have been leasing the property, through Mozhay Point tribal government, from the LaForce descendants, some who have been identified and some who have not. One of the descendants is me, and my descendants are my daughter and her two children.

"Mozhay Point tribal government has offered to purchase Sweetgrass, with plans to build a road along the back ten acres that will connect the tribal center and village with the Miskwaa River State Park. You have offered as part of the purchase agreement to continue my lease that allows me, my daughter, and then my grandchildren to live there for the life of the lease, amending it to update the septic tank and electric, put in a new furnace, build a garage, and blacktop the driveway.

"I am here to say that I not interested in selling the allotment. The lease has almost another seventy years to go, and under the terms that were written down and signed by the council and me, my own descendants will inherit the lease. If I die before my daughter, Crystal Washington Bjornborg, she will inherit the lease, and if she dies before the lease is up, her two children, Joseph and Maggie, will inherit. I have had a will drawn up that restates all of this, and that the children will each inherit half of the shares of Sweetgrass that are mine.

"I know that the tribe could force the sale, but in order to do that, every living descendant of Half-Dime LaForce would have to be located and would have to approve. That would take a very long time—decades, even.

"The road from the tribal buildings to the state park is a rough drive, and once you get past Sweetgrass it can even be dangerous sometimes. A new road to connect to the park, and all the improvements that will be made there with Mozhay, that would be a good thing. And it would eliminate any traffic by the old Odanang settlement, which I think everybody would like to see left undisturbed.

"So I think a new road would be good for everybody. But there are at least two old lumber roads that could be used to build a road from Mesabi to the tribal buildings to the park, not as direct, but they wouldn't involve taking Sweetgrass from our family that has been living there since before there was even a treaty and establishment of the reservation.

"The last thing I want to say is that there are not that many allotments that have stayed in families over the years. The ancestors made a lot of sacrifices for the land, and I think we need to honor that.

"Well, that is all I have to say. Thank you again for allowing me to speak, Chairman Minogeezhik and Representatives Hautala, Simon, Buck, and Washington."

Margie nodded at the mirror, her gray-streaked ponytail bobbing and white bangs flopping over the bows of her glasses, and imagined Jack's response: "Thank you, Ms. Robineau. We will keep your concerns under advisement."

And her dismissal as he smiled in his usual pleasant and unreadable fashion, his triangular eyes shrewd above the reading glasses balanced midway up his formidable-looking nose.

Margie removed Beryl's lucky sweater from its padded hanger in the closet and held it in front of her as she looked again in the mirror. Then she looked at the clock on the bedside table, changed into a sweatshirt and sweatpants, and brushed her teeth. Before getting into bed she carried an old wooden ladder-back chair from the kitchen to the window next to the bed. Kneeling on the chair she opened the window, and the cool night air rolled from the northeast into the room, carrying a light, damp scent of sweetgrass from the sugar bush. From that stand of maples at the far edge of the LaForce allotment where no sweetgrass grew that blessing swirled and drifted with the winds to bless all beings it touched—the animate and inanimate, above and beneath lands and waters.

And the sugar bush is where the body of Zho Wash at last rests, and where it continues the journey toward its destiny, which like ours is to return to the Earth.

Five days before Joey was born, Zho Wash had died in the convalescent care unit at the Mesabi hospital, toward the end of Margie's shift at the casino. From the desk where her name was displayed ("Margie Robineau, Concierge") she watched her son-in-law, Dag, enter through the frosted sliding doors of the entryway, nod to Tom Washington, the security officer, and hurry toward her. From the expression on his face she knew before he spoke, and although Zho's death was not unexpected she looked surprised, Dag thought, her mouth in that little *o* that was the way of the LaForce women as he held her hand and said, "He's gone, Margie."

The plan had been made, by Margie and her daughter, Crystal, that Zho would be buried at Sweetgrass, and so the nursing assistants at convalescent care bathed him and dressed him in clean pajamas before helping Dag gently lift him onto the gurney and into the Mozhay Point ambulance. For the first three days Zho lay in a plain wooden casket in the front room of the house at Sweetgrass while visitors came to stroke Margie's arms, to ask Crystal when the baby was coming, to drop a memento or piece of beadwork into the casket, and to bring cards, money, flowers, and food that Margie's friends set out on the kitchen table. On the fourth day Earl LaForce prayed and spoke, advising Zho's spirit that it was near the end of its arduous journey west and to keep walking. Then the body of Zho Wash—Joseph Washington of the Muskrat dynasty—was buried in the sugar bush, his grave dug and then covered by several strong young Mozhay men. In the tradition of the Muskrat family a stick from a tree branch was pushed into the ground to mark the spot until it fell, through the changes of weather and time, the bark and wood deteriorated, returning to the ground to once again become a part of the Earth, like Zho Wash.

Crystal's baby was born the next day, in the Sweetgrass cabin, delivered by his father, Dag Bjornborg, in the same room in which Crystal had been born. His first visitors were the grandmothers, Margie, Dale Ann, and Grace, and the aunties, Sis and Beryl. Grace, as honored great-grandmother, was given the seat of honor, the rocking chair, and the tiny man placed in her arms. She rocked slowly, gazing at the baby and not speaking at all, while Theresa served tea and cookies and Crystal opened gifts—onesies, diapers, a Minnesota Vikings sleeper, a handmade quilt, and a dreamcatcher.

Beryl declared that he was the handsomest new baby she had ever seen, wondering to herself if Grace was ever going to let someone else hold him. As if she heard, Grace rose from the rocking chair. "Sit here, Dale Ann, and you can hold your little grandson."

"What are you going to call him?" asked Sis, hoping it wouldn't be Dagfinn.

"Dagfinn Joseph Bjornborg. Joey for short," Crystal said. The visitors nodded approvingly.

"You know, I heard that sometimes when one person dies another is born to take their place," said Beryl.

Margie's and Crystal's eyes shone.

Looking out the window in the direction of the sugar bush, Margie breathed in the scent of sweetgrass, then looked up at the sky. She pushed the window down to within an inch of the sill in case of rain, then draped Beryl's sweater over the back of the chair. "Good night, Zho Wash, ni shimose," she said to the photo of the white-haired man on the bedside table.

"Good night, Eva and Lucy," to the two black-and-white photos of his wives: Eva solemn in her Haskell boarding school uniform, and Lucy, laughing, her head thrown back, in front of the aerial bridge in Duluth.

The last picture she looked at was on the wall, an enlarged picture from Margie's phone of her daughter, Crystal, with Crystal's husband, Dag, and their children, Joey and Maggie. "See you soon," she said, then turned off the light and dreamed of Sweetgrass, where Crystal and Dag watched their daughter Maggie fill the bird feeder from the front steps of the LaForce allotment house. They had changed out the kitchen window for one of the kind that stuck out from the house like a box, Margie noticed, approvingly. "Nice place to start seeds in the spring," she said aloud.

The four whose turn it was to watch over Sweetgrass for the night waited for Maggie to finish with the bird feeder, then unfolded their lawn chairs and sat on the grass in front of the deck.

"Isn't that an interesting idea for a window? It will let more light into the kitchen; the house was always so dim." Artense LaForce, wife of Louis, and Margie's great-grandmother, had never liked the allotment house. "That big window in the front room helps, but it's still so much darker than our house over at Odanang." She sniffed, a habit, looking over her large nose at the other ladies who were sitting on lawn chairs in the drive-way. "Don't you agree? Rose, giin dash?"

"More coffee? Made it fresh just before we got here." Rose Sweet, honorary auntie to Margie although not by blood, preferred to be called Sis, but Artense was formal and la-di-da: that was her way. "They've done a lot to the place—when did you move in there, you and your mother and dad, and Henen and Maggie and the baby?"

"Yes, I'll take a warmup. It was a new house built by the government when we moved there, right after Mozhay Point land was divided up in allotments. The Indian agent had Joe Muskrat's house torn down, with the dirt floor. This new one was a board house, with board floors. Our house at Odanang, though, the one everybody called the Etienne house,

was so much bigger. I will admit the house at Sweetgrass was warmer." Artense grimaced slightly at the taste of Sis's coffee. "It had tar paper over the outside walls to keep the wind out. Half-Dime kept fixing it when it tore."

A tiny woman held out a tin cup. "Is that coffee good and strong? I remember when we moved in, Shigogoons. I always thought it was a good house, and I was there longer than anybody else." Therese LaForce, Louis's mother, had outlived both her son and daughter-in-law. "They still have that crucifix hanging on the wall, the one I used to wear. I am glad they decided not to bury it with me." She smoothed the red tape trim on the folded-over top of her dress, as if to touch the silver corpus.

"I've always thought it was lovely," said Beryl Duhlebon, another of Margie's honorary aunties, as she brought her pink china cup to her lips daintily, as was her way. "Margie has always made things look pretty, and she keeps it neat and clean. I liked looking out from the kitchen window of my trailer, watching Margie when she was expecting, and then Crystal growing up. . . . Crystal and Dag took the trailer out after I was gone, which is too bad, because I liked to go inside when I went back to visit, but it really wasn't any good for anybody to live in anymore. And they tore down the outhouse, too. The yard isn't so mucky now; remember how Margie used to have to put on boots to go to the bathroom?" How had Artense kept her dignity going in and out of there?

Artense heard Beryl's thought. "It was much dryer then. Half-Dime kept things in good repair, I will say that for him. And the outhouse was there when we got there, not Louis's doing. The privy he built at our house in Odanang, now that was properly done, drainage under the walkway, and the holes must have been dug thirty feet deep."

"This house, and the allotment, she knows what it means, Margie—to us, to Zho Wash, and the Muskrats. This is not going to be easy for her." Therese opened the tanned deerskin pouch tied at her waist and took out a white clay pipe and a bag of tobacco. Tamping a pinch into the bowl she lit a match and inhaled; the tobacco sparked and lit. Smoke rose into the night sky, over Dag, Crystal, and their daughter Maggie, over the house and the Sweetgrass allotments. Therese, Artense, Sis, and Beryl gazed at the stars, pondering the past and the present, offering their prayers for the future.

Until morning, when Margie woke, the ladies drank coffee as they thought and prayed, with the exception of Artense, whose gift from the Creator was that she thought and thought.

St. Louis County Road 5 runs westward some thirty miles from the border town of Mesabi to the Miskwaa River State Park, where it ends. Halfway to the park an old, rarely used road branches off next to the Dionne family house and allotment land: that intersection, the Dionne Fork, marks the southeastern boundary of the Mozhay Point Band of Chippewa reservation.

Across from the Dionne house is the Aadabaaning! Mozhay Point Gas & Grocery, previously the Tuomela Gas & Grocery Skelly Station, purchased by the tribal government when the elderly couple who owned it retired. Speed bumps slow traffic at the complex of tribal office buildings and over the next mile or so at the entrances to the Chi Waabik casino, motel, and golf course, the Head Start and elementary school building, and again five miles farther west at Minwendaming, the elder housing apartments, built on the south shore of Lost Lake.

From the Dionne Fork to the state park, the rest of County 5 has been known to locals since the land allotment days as "the road to Sweetgrass." County 5 has been black-topped since not long after the casino began to show a profit and is kept plowed and patched by Mozhay Point Facilities. Past Minwendaming, houses are occasional and scattered, some set very close to the road and some three or four hundred feet back, the only indication of their existence the domed steel mailboxes at the end of the driveways. In recent years, however, new houses have gone up, quite different from the old allotment shacks built a hundred years ago or the prefabs flung up in the 1970s; the new houses are large, some with landscaping and lawns clipped and styled as though by a hairdresser, their septic systems dug to accommodate twice the size of the houses and described by Margie's daughter, Crystal, the Mozhay Point Director of Health Services, as "top-notch and failproof."

The road grows more narrow and winding as it proceeds west: midway between the Dionne Fork and the Miskwaa River State Park is Sweetgrass, the LaForce family allotment lands, first passing the empty spot where Beryl Duhlebon's turquoise trailer once stood, and next the allotment house, built by the government for Half-Dime LaForce when their family had been assigned the land. The Muskrat family, renamed the Washingtons by the Indian agent, were removed from Sweetgrass and allowed to live on the half-mile strip next to the Miskwaa River as unallotted and unrecognized Indians. Aandakii Anishinaabeg, they called themselves: the original, good people who had been created by the Great Spirit and gently lowered to the Earth. And then displaced to live elsewhere.

Perhaps a quarter-mile past Sweetgrass is the boat

landing on Lost Lake, busy during ricing season. From there the road narrows farther, in some places to one lane, in some nearly overgrown by the brush that wills its way to cover any access.

Not far from the abandoned DWP railroad tracks that mark the western end of Mozhay, and not visible from the road, are the ruins of the former American Fur Post and Odanang settlement, the no-man's-land that is the abandoned former home of the Muskrat family that was renamed by the Indian agent as well as other unallotted Indians who had not signed the land cession treaty that created the reservation boundaries, in both land and citizenship. Finally, the road opens to daylight and the cleared entrance to the state park visitor and parking lot, and it is there that the road ends.

The visitors' center is a log-sided one-story prefab built in the 1980s with labor from the Mozhay Point Band; inside are the park ranger's office, a gift shop, and concessions. On the side of the parking lot is a railed observation platform from which Mozhay Pointers and visitors can look down at the Miskwaa Rapids and the inlet where canoes had loaded and unloaded more than a century and a half ago. Hiking trails lead to the Miskwaa Rivertrail in one direction and in the other to Half-Dime Hill, the outcropping of gabbro rock covered with eons of earth, trees, and brush that is just east of the river and the old settlement.

Afterwards, whenever Margie thought about the day the boy was found, the one nobody had known was lost, she would remember first the sky over the northwest corner of Sweetgrass, blue as deep as a juniper berry, and Theresa's hair, strands of lavender gray breeze-borne from her outstretched palm to float over the sleepy rapids of the Miskwaa River.

Margie had left her house in Sweetgrass that morning with her teenage grandson, Joey, to drive him the five miles to the Miskwaa River State Park visitor center where he worked as a cashier, clerk, and washroom attendant, and to meet her friend Theresa for coffee and frybread at the concession stand. Joey turned the car radio low to the station that played his kind of music, lyrics that Margie hoped she couldn't understand; she opened the windows and he turned the radio off.

"The air smells like fall today, like sun on yellow leaves, or maybe more like cowslips when the sun shines down into the swamp," Margie commented. "On the back side of the allotment, next to the sugar bush. Aniin ikidowin fall, ningoozins?"

"Dagwaagin," said Joey. "Starts like summer and ends like winter, with football season in the middle. You going to the game tomorrow night? Home game at Mesabi."

"Amanj, depends. Dale Ann might be coming over to watch a movie. If I don't go, you can take the Jeep."

Joey smiled, immediately making plans to himself.

"*If* you get home by eleven. To your mom and dad's, I mean; you can keep the Jeep overnight." Her plan was to invite Joey's other grandmother, Dale Ann Minogeezhik, to the cabin at Sweetgrass to watch *The Way We Were* on TCM and pump Dale Ann for anything she could tell her about the tribe's plans to acquire Sweetgrass, the LaForce family allotment lands. Dale Ann's husband Jack, longtime Mozhay tribal chair, shared quite a lot of confidential information with her; some of this she in turn shared with Margie, as long as Margie kept things to herself and didn't let on that she knew.

I'll get out that bottle of Moscato, Margie thought to herself. Dale Ann likes that. Maybe I'll ask Theresa to come, too, though she can't drink these days, of course. She likes Robert Redford.

Along both sides of the road, the yellowing green of birch leaves and the brilliance of maple leaves, yellows, oranges, and reds, flashed past, interspersed with the year-round greens of pines. The car approached the curve after Lost Lake boat landing and ricing camp, Margie braking as the blacktopped surface ended and the road narrowed. Stands of trees thickened, and beneath the density of white pines the sun disappeared, and Margie turned on the head-lights. The road dipped, rose, dipped for a few miles as Margie concentrated, steering left, right, left, around puddles of standing water that had eroded the dirt to potholes.

"Grandma, remember when I used to ask you if there were monsters in the woods when we came by here?" asked Joey.

"*Monchers,* you asked if there were *monchers,* then you'd do this shivery thing with your fingers on each side of your face." Margie smiled. "Remember that?"

"Like this?" Joey bared his teeth and made a chewing motion, wiggling his fingers up and down from his eye-brows to his chin.

"Scare-ree!" said Margie, laughing.

"But do you think there are, really, Grandma? Like in the old stories?"

"Nobody knows. I don't know of anybody who has ever seen one, not really." How much to tell him? "The old people always say to be careful in the woods, that there are animals and spirits who live there, it's their home."

"But do you think there are?"

"Amanj I dash, Joey; I don't know. I just always remember what the old people have said, the stories about the world, how things came to be and the good ways to act."

Both in thought, Margie and her grandson looked at the trees and deep woods that as they drove closer to Odanang edged closer and closer around the car until they were driving through a twilit tunnel. Waiting for the sun to return, Joey thought to himself how he hated this part of the road and turned the radio back on, this time looking for Margie's country station. He whistled tunelessly, wondering if this might be the time the darkness of the woods prevailed permanently over any light of day, and the car would drive in twilight until it ran out of gas. And then, as always happened, the trees suddenly cleared. They passed the large rustic-looking wooden sign that read "Miskwaa River State Park: Site of Historic American Fur Company Trading Post and Odanang Village" and drove into the parking lot.

"We're first ones here, beat Theresa, as usual, and you're early for work," Margie said as she pulled into the row of spaces near the door marked "Reserved for Elders" and turned off the ignition. "It's because I've got a lead foot." She looked at her watch. Ten minutes to spend with her grandson, who next to her daughter, Crystal, was the dearest person on Earth to her.

"Do you know what you'll be doing for work today?"

"I'm supposed to count the inventory in the supply room and make a report—and keep an eye on the bathrooms. Easy. Inventory is running down."

Because of the healthy number of tourists in that brief, profitable holdover from the summer camping and hiking season, the visitor center overlooking the gentle Miskwaa River maintains a stock of T-shirts, mugs, books about the natural world, and children's toys—small, hard rubber bears, wolves, and eagles—which sell steadily until after the leaves have fallen and the freeze sets in. Before the muddy road from Sweetgrass has frozen into deep, snow-covered ruts, the facility will close for the season and left-over stocked packed and moved to the basement of the Chi Waabik casino.

In winter, the road from Sweetgrass is impassable, the closed park resting under a heavy blanket of snow. The chained entrance will guard the seasonal sleep that lasts every year into spring, when the snow and ground begin to melt, freeze, and melt again into a fecund muckiness more than a foot deep. Still impassible, the road guards the earth that will grow life to dense greenery, and finally a drying that will allow for the road to be graded once again. In this way, weather and climate, as preordained by the Creator, replenish natural resources and renew the spirit of terrain and river, and those beings of body and spirit who live there in and out of tourist season, and in the past and present.

This will all change, however, if the Mozhay Point Economic Development Committee prevails with the tribal council: in a partnership with the state of Minnesota, the road from Sweetgrass would become only a secondary route to the park. Two old, unused lumber roads that run along the northern border of the reservation and near the tribal administration buildings, housing complex, school, and casino will be reopened and paved, straightened, and linked across the Sweetgrass allotment lands, and the park will be redesigned to include an indoor-outdoor winter sports complex.

The connected lumber roads would need straightening in just one area: the northern ten acres of Sweetgrass, the LaForce family allotment lands. The proceeds from the sale of any of the allotment land must by law be divided among several dozen LaForce relatives; however, Margie, as the oldest child of the oldest child of the oldest child of the original allotment holder, will have final voice on the sale. She intends to live on the allotment at Sweetgrass until she dies, at which point Crystal would inherit Margie's share of the allotment as well as the position of deciding to sell or not. Margie has told Crystal that she has no intention of selling the allotment land, in its entirety or piece by piece.

On that breezy lavender-juniper-marigold morning not long after the brilliance of autumn colors has peaked but still within tourist season, Margie Robineau, Sweetgrass heiress who stands in the way of progress and tribal economic development, talks with her grandson in her decade-old dusty-gray Jeep Liberty passing the time before he begins work for the day.

"Just a few more weeks left before closing. Are you going to try to get the same job next year?"

"I like it, but what I'm hoping is to be one of the park ranger assistants; they mostly clean trails and around the outside and pick up after anybody who doesn't clean up after themselves on the grounds around the building, but sometimes they get to run errands and do other things to help, too. It would be good experience for what I want to do when I finish college, be a park ranger, like Scott Martin."

College. A park ranger. Margie beamed. "Maybe you'll be the park ranger here after Scott retires."

"But *today*, it's inventory and bathrooms. Miigwan's working the counter and the phone; I think she wanted inventory, but they gave it to me to do."

"They must think you're good at it."

The boy smiled proudly and shrugged. "I think Merrilee's coming," he said. "Is that them?"

A late-model Ford Transit van with the Mozhay Point Band of Ojibwe logo decaled on each side, and above that "Council of Elders," has emerged from the denseness of the road from Sweetgrass and parks next to the Jeep.

"Almost time; guess I better go in. Thanks for the ride, Grandma. I'll find a ride home."

Margie's eyes loved on the sight of her grandson's soft, wavy hair, his dark blue-brown eyes so like his mother's, and his rather toothy, brilliant smile. "Well, call me if you don't and I'll come pick you up," she replied, then, "Joey, don't forget your hat."

"Oh, yeah." The boy took the mesh cap from Margie's hand and pulled it neatly onto his head, feeling for the exact placement above each ear, checking for the exact center of the visor and the exact center of his hairline. The words, yellow on green, "Miskwaa River" with "Historical State Park" on the line below were exactly parallel with the level ground of the parking lot. "Migwech! Is it straight, Grandma?"

"Very handsome!" This from the woman who had parked the van next to Margie's Jeep.

The boy grinned, open-mouthed, his hair springing from either side of his head below the green hat. "Hi, Auntie Merrilee; Boozhoo, Auntie Theresa, Uncle Michael."

The men shook hands. "What time is work?" asked Michael.

"Five minutes."

"You call if you need a ride home after, eh."

"I will, Uncle." Joey walked up the wooden deck stairs to the back door into the staff room. He raised one hand before entering the building. "See youse," he called. "Gi gawaabimin!"

The elders waved.

*

"Let's find a table, Ma, for you and Auntie Margie; Dad and I will get your coffee." Merrilee led, and her usual rapid walk slowed to match the speed of the three. Theresa took her husband's arm with one hand and steadied the chemotherapy pack that was strapped bandolier-style across her chest with the other, stepping cautiously but surprisingly deftly under the burden, tubing looped over her arm and fingers.

Michael, his lumbering bear walk thoughtful, slowly shifted the weight of his chest, shoulders, and stomach, imperceptibly heavier each year since he was twenty but now accrued over five decades to an exaggerated bulkiness over his much smaller hips and legs precarious in its side-to-side movement with each step. Behind the couple, Margie carried her purse, Theresa's tote bag, and a fleece blanket—cautious in her own gait, feet in Birkenstock sandals and thick socks carefully choosing each step, nearly soundless over the pea gravel path and below the whir of insect songs and leaves that quivered in the wake of Merrilee's strong and confident steps.

Pretty shoes, Margie thought looking toward Theresa's feet in lavender and silver ASICS. *They match her hair.*

Theresa held her husband's arm; Margie's eyes moved, as they did invariably when she thought he wouldn't notice, to Michael's broad back, thick black hair shot through with silver strands; she sighed at his strutting, slightly bowlegged walk. *Wijiiwagan, still partners and still the best-looking couple in the whole Minnesota Chippewa Tribe,* she continued to herself. *And all grown up, that Merrilee; she was always such a nice little girl the way she took care of all the younger kids, and she still is.*

On the deck outside the concession stand Theresa's nice

little girl strode firmly around a group of tourists toward the table that was cleanest and most sheltered from wind and sun, then helped Michael to seat her mother comfortably. "Merrilee, why don't you see what your mother and Margie want from the stand while we're out on the trails; I'm going to talk with Scott about something," said Michael. "Won't take long, then we can go check some things out. You good with that, Theresa?"

"That's why I wanted to come along; we were going to have a visit."

Theresa asked for tea, Margie for coffee. "And maybe something to go with it," requested Theresa. "Anything they've got ready."

"I'll be right back!"

"Take your time."

"You think the place looks as good as it did before they fixed it up?" asked Theresa.

"Well, it's different; but you know? It was pretty before and it's pretty now. I'm not crazy about the parking lot, but if you don't really look at that, it's a lot the same. And there's bathrooms!" Both women laughed. "And at the edge of the patio, that nice railing you can lean on and hang on to when you look at the river and down at the inlet—when I do that, I think they must look like they probably did a hundred years ago."

"I wonder how it will look after they add all the improvements; they say it will look even more natural than it does now." Theresa wondered where she might work the purchase of Sweetgrass and the connecting road across the allotment land into the conversation.

Margie didn't reply.

Theresa continued: "Remember the day we came up

here to meet Zho Wash and went with Michael to check his snares?"

It was the first time Margie had ever seen Michael. "Yes, we were driving that Nova of yours." The white Nova had belonged to Theresa's mother, who instead of trading it in when she bought a VW Rabbit had given it to her daughter. A student at the college in Duluth, Theresa had been a generous car owner, driving Margie to the grocery store, to the mall, to powwows—she kept a dozen blankets and quilts in the trunk so they always had a comfortable place to sleep, even in the car—and one time to the Mozhay Point reservation, to see a boy she had met at school, Michael Washington. The scene played in Margie's memory, Michael waiting for the Nova in front of the gas station, smoking a cigarette, the wind whipping his long hair into black strings. He had taken a last drag on the cigarette and tossed it into a snowbank, called, "See you, Dale Ann!" to a young woman inside the gas station who was cleaning the window, and got into the back seat of the car, in back of Margie. He smelled of snow and cigarettes, and his attention was on Theresa, who pushed aside the curtain of her hair to introduce him to Margie.

"So, Margie, what have you been thinking about the council's offer to buy Sweetgrass?"

"I'm going to tell them I'm not interested."

"That must be so hard, your family's allotment, but then when you think of all the great things that can happen for everybody, the land, and the tribe, and you and your kids . . ."

"Holy, did you come here to have coffee or to work on me?"

"To visit with you. I'm sorry. Hey, remember we didn't

sleep in the Nova when we came up to meet Michael, but we slept in it a lot of times; that was one great car. Remember when we drove from Duluth to the spring powwow at Mozhay and we left the trunk open and it rained?"

"That Nova was a good car. When you finally sold it, you got $200 from Eugene, and he got another five years out of it."

"Sleeping in the Nova, going to the bathroom in the outhouses next to the powwow grounds. Did you ever think that one day we would be old ladies who appreciated a nice bathroom with a flush toilet?"

Both women laughed. "The patio and the overlook are really nice; you can just sit here and look across the river. Do you want to move closer to the rail, look down at the inlet?"

Theresa mused: "You know what would be nice to have when they fix this place up more would be putting a fur post replica in, maybe even rebuilding part of Odanang, like the fur post at Thunder Bay. Can you picture Indians and fur traders paddling up to the inlet, there?"

The inlet below the guardrail had once served as the harbor for a small fur trading post and settlement of Ojibwe people across the Miskwaa River from the small-scale, gentle rapids bubbling over the shallow, rocky western shore. Never lucrative, the fur post did not really prosper even during the demand for furs in Europe and North America; by the time the 1854 land cession treaty was signed and the Mozhay Point reservation borders established, the fur post had been closed. Those Miskwaa River dwellers who signed the treaty were removed to Mozhay Point; those who did not, which included the honorable Muskrat family later named the Washingtons, were removed to a half-mile strip on the eastern banks of the Miskwaa, just above the rapids, where the fur post and community remained only as buildings that over time eroded and collapsed, returning to the earth, and the ghosts of the old Miskwaa River dwellers.

"We should get Dale Ann out here for coffee one of these days," said Margie. "She has told me she's getting ready to retire; she could take a morning to come here and visit with us. All those people she has working in education take care of everything: the scholarship programs, the elementary school, Head Start and preschool, grant writing. She oversees the department and the budget, but she's always run a tight ship. She could take things a little easier."

"I could go give her a call right now; should I do that? I doubt she'd come; she's married not only to the tribal chair but to her job."

"I think there's more to it, though," said Margie, "don't you? She met us just last week in the coffee shop at Chi Waabik. When's the last time she was ever out here at the park?"

"She kept her cell phone right there on the table, next to her bannock—don't you love their bannock, the way they serve it warm, with all that butter melting on top? She's never been much for outdoors, Dale Ann hasn't. Not for things like Merrilee's groups, but she did make that little sweetgrass basket when we did crafts. That was outside, remember?"

"Under a tent canopy, and in the wildflower garden next to the restaurant."

"Well, she is kind of a glamour girl," said Theresa, "careful to stay out of the sun. But I know what you mean."

"Mmm hmm," Margie nodded. "Ever since I can remember she has always had a reason to not go out to Miskwaa."

"Should I go call her? She should see for herself, not just on those plans on paper, where things will be if the year-round facilities go through. Heated buildings, air conditioning, good plumbing . . ."

"You're still trying to work me, aren't you? You see that truck there, the busted-down-looking red one, see the bumper sticker? Well, that's how it's going to be with the allotment land; they're going to have to pry it out of my cold, dead fingers."

"Well, okay, then. Hey, look, they're coming with gapii-donut!"

Merrilee and Michael returned, Merrilee carrying a cardboard tray and Michael a heavy paper plate. "Here's your coffee, Margie; milk and sugar, and your tea, Ma. Frybread's not ready yet—Dad said you'd both like plain doughnuts, right?"

Michael asked if Theresa was warm enough and left his jacket hanging on the back of her chair in case she felt chilled while he was away. "You going to be all right here? Want anything else, a piece of frybread when it's ready? We can wait."

Theresa leaned back into the warm bow of Michael's chest. "We're fine sitting until you get back, and we can have lunch then from the stand. We're good here; me and Margie have a lot of catching up to do—it's been days, right, Margie?"

"Days and days!"

"Okay, then," Michael said, "back in about half an hour. We're going over past the old settlement and then around the side of the hill to the lumber road, to take some pictures, for the council meeting."

"You need anything, Ma, somebody in the center will keep an eye out to help you; just wave and they'll see you. Remember, if you want to use your phones or get on the internet you'll need to go inside to use the wifi. Gawd, I wish they had cell service besides in that building."

"What do you think we'd want to call anybody for? A lot of fuss going on here."

Michael lightly squeezed Theresa's shoulders and kissed the top of her head. "See you soon," he said.

"Maajaa daa, Dad," said Merrilee, "if we want to get back in time for lunch."

A scene from decades ago played across Theresa's memory, Merrilee outside of Michael's office window in the reservation business building. She tapped on the window; laughing, she turned a cartwheel on the grass. "Merrilee! Can you still do a cartwheel?" Theresa asked.

Merrilee obliged. "Yup." Walking away, her voice carried back to the table. "Well, when they put in the new road they're really going to need to get a cell tower, Dad. Do you know, is anybody on Planning talking about that?"

Margie shifted her chair closer to Theresa's, inhaling the faintness of warmth and scent left by Michael, who had disappeared into the sumac leaves that half-obscured the beginning of the hiking trail. "They're so funny together, aren't they? All into tribal politics. I suppose Merrilee will run for council one of these days. What kind of tea is that? It smells like hay."

Theresa tore open a packet of sugar and stirred it into the cup, took a sip, and wrinkled her nose. "Something herbal . . . probably. It's about all she ever talks about, politics and her work," she said, her thoughts not on Mozhay Point business but on her middle-aged daughter who had yet to show an interest in marrying.

"I heard that she had coffee with John Ricebird and Fred Simon at the Forest last week." Margie had been thinking about Merrilee, too.

Theresa half-sighed. "They were talking about funding an outing for the women in Ladyslipper House—you know, the group home in Duluth that Fred Simon's daughter-in-law Azure Gallette runs? He told her the Cultural Center can give them a tour and put together a craft program, and buy their lunch at the Forest buffet. John said he would help."

"Well, that will take some planning—and I think John looks like a lonely guy sometimes, and who knows where working together on something like this could lead?"

"You could be right about that: who knows?" Theresa wound the end of her braid around her index finger, looking hopeful. In thought, she watched a hawk circle the top of Half-Dime Hill in the blue October sky, blinking at a silvery glint of light that flashed brilliantly for less than a second halfway down the hill and then disappeared.

Balanced on a rock ledge halfway to the peak of Half-Dime Hill, a couple argued about the steepness of the climb, the absurdity of any further attempt to get to the top, and the fate of a lidded silver carafe. Their pyramid-shaped sun hats, contraptions draped and suspended over wicker forms that rose inches above their heads, quivered and swayed in the discussion. Would a hill in a state park, overlooking the ruins of an abandoned fur post and village near a reservation, suffice for the wish of the deceased to be sprinkled over an ancient Indian burial ground?

"Fine, it's an old Indian burial ground, then, whatever, Lyle," said the woman. "Go ahead, then: open it up and shake it out but for God's sake be careful," and she steadied herself by grabbing a branch of the small cedar tree growing nearby from a crack in the rock. Looking away as the man worked the silver lid free from the carafe, she watched the current of the slow-moving Miskwaa River below reflect the October sun back to the sky, both soon to be joined by the cremains that would scatter and drift, the lightest and most powdery floating into the atmosphere, some blown from the hill to the river, and the rest falling to the ground below, dust to dust.

And some perhaps falling onto the two women below on the observation deck overlooking the river, one seated and one standing, unaware that their existence might soon coincide with the ashes of a no-longer-living visitor to the Historic Miskwaa River State Park. Were they some of the local Indian tribe, the canvas-hatted woman wondered? With her free hand she lifted the binoculars that hung from a strap around her neck and, unable to use her other hand to focus, squinted and the scene cleared.

The seated woman, Theresa Washington, loosened the long braid that hung over one shoulder and combed her fingers through her gray hair that glowed with a slight lavender tint in the sunlight. Strands of hair, some thick and some thin, dripped from her fingers; caught by the breeze they floated over the guard railing and into the river, winding and unwinding, undulating and rebraiding into the current. The standing woman, Margie Robineau, opened her purse and took out a hairbrush; she tenderly gathered and coaxed Theresa's remaining hair into a ponytail that she looped back onto itself to a silver-lavender oval that hung down her back.

The man pried at the carafe's tightly sealed lid that seemed to be stuck. Swearing softly, he tried to insert his car key into the lid and twist. The lid stayed sealed.

"Bev, help me out here. I'll hold the urn with both hands and you try turning the key."

Bev sighed as she twisted the key in the edge of the seal. "Nothing. For God's sake, Roger ..."

At the top of the hill, tiny Teresa LaForce stood in the shadow cast by her tall daughter-in-law sucking calmly on her clay pipe. "I believe it's time, my dear," she said, holding out a small, round pebble.

Artense rolled the pebble between her palms and took the stance she had earlier in the morning, turned slightly to the right with her left shoulder, foot leading. She inhaled deeply through her long nose and narrowed her eyes; her mouth formed into that thoughtful little o-shape, she exhaled slowly and shifted her weight to her left foot as she pitched the stone, which hit the lid of the urn with a silvery ping!

... that loosed the top of the urn with a pop, startling a chipmunk who had been watching from above the man's head. The chipmunk fled, loosening sand beneath a larger stone that rolled down to bounce off the man's canvas hat, which quivered. He jumped, body and hat shaking in horror as cremains dust rose in a cloud from the open urn, then lost his balance, shuffling his feet in the loose soil of the ledge, which separated and gave way. Throwing both arms around his wife's waist he shouted her name like a question, "Bev?" as he dropped the silver carafe, which slid and bounced down Half-Dime Hill, the freed cremains of the departed joining the shattered pieces of rock ledge and a rolling, growing wave of small trees, bushes, rocks, and earth, and the departed.

The couple clung to each other and the small cedar, which remained rooted in a cracked rock on eroding Half-Dime Hill. "Help! He-e-e-e-lp!" the woman called, her voice swallowed by a breeze that wound like ribbons through the tamaracks and jack pines and the gentle sound of the slow-moving Miskwaa Rapids, water taking its own sweet time in the wearing down of stones.

Below, Margie and Theresa sat on the observation deck over the river, waiting for the day's first batch of frybread from the concession stand. "Bekong boweting," commented Margie. "I wonder why they call it a rapids."

"Must be something in translation," answered Theresa. "Ojibwe to English, words don't always match up."

"A rapids doesn't have to be fast, geget."

"Remember when that new guy at the golf shack was in a hurry to get off work and told the caddies he had to book it?" Theresa snorted, then dabbed her eyes and blew her nose on the handkerchief she kept tucked into her jacket sleeve.

"Lost and found in translation; they'll never let him forget that! Oh, look at that; I laughed so hard I spilled my coffee!" Margie mopped at the puddle on the table with a napkin.

"Shh, listen." Theresa turned her face toward Half-Dime Hill. "Do you hear something? What is that??"

"It sounds like 'Hello-o-o-o, hello-o-o-o' coming from the hill."

"Look! Coming from the trail—it's Merrilee, and she's starting to run! What's wrong?" asked Theresa and called her daughter's name across the parking lot.

Hearing her mother's worried voice, Merrilee, her mouth open wide and gulping air, attempted to compose her panicked face. Distracted by her failure to do that, she half-walked and half-ran toward the visitor center, tripping and landing on her hands and knees in the graveled path.

the scattering

EARLIER THAT MORNING, a Subaru Outback had pulled into the visitor center parking lot, its rear bumper barely missing one of the grounds crew when the driver backed up to be closer to the trail entrance. The unseen grounds worker jumped out of the way and tapped on the rear passenger door; unaware, the driver braked, turned off the ignition, and opened the door. Still seated, he was framed by the open car door: an older man dressed in a white long-sleeved shirt and khaki pants that hiked up, exposing heavy tan hiking socks below shiny, hairless shins that gleamed white in the sunlight.

"Roger, your skin, your skin." The passenger, a woman in a shirt and pants that matched his, semi-rolled out from her side of the car and reached inside, ducking from the sun. "Pull down your pants legs," she ordered as she stepped, more limber than her husband, out the passenger door. "The sun is almost right overhead, such a glare; get your sun hat on right away," she instructed and crowned herself with a large canvas, tentlike form with a frame structure inside that suspended the fabric to a floating mushroom that obscured her entire head except for a cutout in front. She donned gloves, then sunglasses, then helped the man secure his hat, like hers but somewhat larger and wider, with the slider under his chin. The mushroom people hoisted back-packs, which they secured with buckles at the front of their chests and waists, and plodded grimly onto the hiking trail.

Theresa sputtered into her tea. "Holy," she said.

"What in the hell?" said Margie. "They might as well stay inside."

Margie and Theresa were quiet for a moment.

"Do you think Merrilee gets lonely?" Theresa asked.

"Well, she's so busy with everything she does: her camping groups, her job at the RBC, not to mention driving people around in the Council of Elders van—when would she find the time?"

"I think that might be why she fills up her days like that, because she is lonely. Fred Simon, since Lillian died, it must be hard for him—and he's such a good man. He's too old for Merrilee, though. Way too old."

"Oh, you think so?" Margie raised her eyebrows and clicked her tongue.

Theresa remembered that Joe Washington, whom Margie had lived with at Sweetgrass since she was twenty, had been older than Margie's own father.

"Remember how she was born," Margie continued. "With a caul. We don't know yet what that means for her."

Theresa had been told how magical this was, but she had not seen any indication of mystical inclinations in her daughter. She scratched her head, her scalp crawling; she wondered what that might have to do with her starting to lose her hair. Was each hair hanging on desperately, trying to corkscrew itself into her scalp, all in vain as they fell one by one to drape, singly or in twos or threes, on her shoulders?

"I'm going to see if there's any hikers down by the inlet," Margie said and crossed the patio to the stone guardrail at the edge of the overlook. Leaning, she watched the waters of the Miskwaa River inlet churn as gently as they had every year from April through October since long before the fur post and settlement, both abandoned a century ago. "Getting cooler," she said to herself. "Leaves are falling fast; a month from now we'll see snow." She squinted at the sun dazzling on the slowly undulating waves and turned toward the picnic table to wave at Theresa. "Nobody there!" she called, then leaned again over the inlet, sprinkling a small handful of tobacco, damp from her left palm, into the water. She dusted her hands together over the water and walked back to the table.

"Theresa," called a woman from the concession stand. "Michael and Merrilee were going to wait, but the dough isn't made yet so they decided to go on the Half-Dime Trail. They said they'll be back in about twenty minutes. I hope Michael can keep up with her! They told me to get you more coffee and tea if you want it. And donuts. Just say if you want some."

"If she is keeping an eye on things, she's a little slow," Theresa muttered and raised her voice to call back "Migwech, Shirl—we're going to wait and eat lunch when they get back. Mino gizheb, eh? Nice morning!"

"Sure is! You want more hot water or to warm your coffee? Made a fresh pot!"

"We're still good, Shirl!"

Theresa looked Margie fully in the face, a small line between her eyebrows deepening. "So, I don't know. Merrilee looks tired sometimes to me. Do you see that?"

"That Merrilee—she can probably carry Michael back here if he gets tired out! Is she still doing those Women in the Wilderness canoe trips?"

"Not for long; once it snows Chi Waabik is going to have these winter camping trips this year. She'll lead those."

"Winter camping—geez, just like the old-time Mozhay Pointers, eh?" Both women laughed, and Margie blew on her coffee to cool it.

"Theresa," Margie asked, "sure you don't want to sit by the guardrail to see be-kaaning, the rapids? It looks like diamonds down there, bouncing off the waves."

"Do I need to hurry?"

"Wewiib, bimibitoon; you never know when the old be-kaaning might decide to speed up!"

Both women laughed at the old Mozhay Pointer joke that called the rapids "the slow place."

"Give me a second." Theresa Washington looked at seventy much like she had at twenty, when she was Theresa Dooley: on the tall side, slender, broad-shouldered, and skinny in the haunch. However, since her illness her walk had become ever so slightly cautious and somewhat unsteady, and her hair, that at twenty had draped nearly to her waist, a dark chestnut curtain that swayed and dipped in rhythm to her confident step, at seventy hung from the nape of her neck in a slender braid, light gray in color but glinting lavender highlights under the sun, this from the purple Silver Fox shampoo she washed it with twice a week.

"You know, let me finish my tea first. It was so godawful hot. It's finally cool enough to drink. Is your coffee still warm?" Theresa gently tapped the side of Margie's cup with one hand, with the other delicately holding the tubing that led to a toxic cocktail with a life of its own slowly coursing from the chemotherapy pack that hung over one shoulder to the placket on her shirt, where it disappeared between the buttons to the port implanted over her heart.

They drank their coffee in the comfortable and familiar ease of a half-century of friendship, Margie unaware that her lips were moving in prayer between sips and unaware that Theresa watched her. The wind picked up and dried maple leaves danced from the concession stand and across the cement walkway of the overlook; reaching the guardrail they piled up, trapped.

"I was thinking I might cut my hair," said Theresa. "Something easier to take care of, maybe a bob . . . What do you think? It doesn't really stay in the braid; the shorter pieces just slide right out after awhile, it's getting so thin."

"Not so thin that anybody would notice, but gray hair does have a mind of its own," said Margie, thinking that Theresa's hair had always been so much a part of who she was. Of course, she would be the same Theresa without it, wouldn't she? Margie's short ponytail and thick bangs were the same style they had been for decades. "Mine would stick out all over the place, but I just use a little water to smooth it down. Works most of the time. For awhile, anyway."

"I was thinking of something like Dale Ann's hair."

Margie tried to picture Theresa with the same hair as Dale Ann's—feathered and sprayed, any wayward strays or strands sternly welded into the scallops that rose like rough waves from the morning's comb-out. "I don't know. Dale Ann's hair looks like a lot of work."

"You know what I mean, though, see?" Theresa pulled her braid forward over her shoulder and rolled the elastic band from the end. As she combed her fingers through the braid, long pale lavender-gray hairs escaping the confines of the braid separated; some settled on the purple fleece of her jacket and others wafted away in the October breeze; out of sight they floated over the overlook, the picnic tables, the guardrail, and down toward the slow rapids of the Miskwaa River. "Yi, just look at that. Bugat, that's all I can say."

"Want me to braid it up again for you, maybe a French braid that starts at the top of your head? I won't do it tight."

"Could you just put it in a ponytail low at the back for now?"

Margie gently and carefully gathered her friend's hair. Facing away from the rapids, she took in the view of Half-Dime Hill in autumn as it had been for as long as the rapids had gently rolled in the Miskwaa River inlet, pine trees and brush sprouting at odd angles from the uneven masses of gabbrous rock, formed eons ago and still forming and re-forming as cracked stone shifted under its own weight and fell.

"Concession stand's getting busy. The gift shop should do a good business on a beautiful day like today," she remarked, winding the hair back onto itself. She would wrap the pony-tail into a loop, prettier than the hair just hanging down. "Wait till you see what I'm doing; the back of your head will look like a silver horseshoe."

"Maybe I'll get it cut in a bob. Or maybe just wear a scarf."

"You start wearing scarves and everybody else will start wearing scarves, too." Margie had always thought that Theresa was the coolest girl she knew.

"Parking lot is getting full, too, almost lunchtime for tourists. I guess they love their frybread. Did you see that it's five dollars for one piece at the stand? Tourists don't care; Joey will make some tip money today." Theresa squinted toward Half-Dime Hill. "Do you see people on the hill? Crazy hikers who don't read the signs? I can't quite see— I think it's those people in the big white hats."

"Where's the rubber band" Margie asked, the doubled-up silver ponytail in one hand.

"Look, Merrilee's coming back. She's running!" Theresa rose, her head pulling against Margie's snapping of the rubber band into the loop of hair. "What is she doing by herself?"

"Maybe somebody went past the signs and got lost on the trails. Maybe that pair in the big sun hats." Margie squinted at Half-Dime Hill. "No, they're still there, not moving up or down. Maybe they're stuck. Couple of boobs." She looped Theresa's hair twice through the elastic rubber band. "There. How does that feel?"

"Some people think those signs don't apply to them—but why would Merrilee be running?"

Trotting with her short-legged, muscular stride from the base of Half-Dime Hill toward the visitor center, Merrilee bumped a recycling bin with one hip but stayed on her feet. "Excuse me, excuse me," she said to a young mother pushing a baby stroller. "Sorry, sorry," she muttered as she nearly stepped on a small boy holding a rubber moose, just purchased from the gift shop. The boy peered from under the u-shaped visor of his Minnesota Twins baseball hat.

"Mom," he asked the woman with the stroller, "is that an Indian?"

Merrilee tripped and stumbled, landing on her hands and knees. On all fours, she shook her head, blinked, and shook her head again.

It was surprising how quickly Theresa could move, feet in lavender ASICS that matched her hair hardly making a sound above the whir of insect wings and leaves quivering in the wake of Merrilee's run and fall. What was the last thing she had said to her daughter, her muscular, middle-aged, childless daughter whom she loved above all else, before—before what? Theresa shook her head, the loop of the silver horseshoe loosening. Oh, yes: "Can you still do a cartwheel?"

Margie, her right arm around Theresa's waist and her right hand holding the clear plastic loop of chemo pack tubing, matched steps with her friend, the two in a three-legged race faster than the slow Miskwaa Rapids.

Merrilee raised her head and shook it, disoriented.

"Let me help you up; are you all right?" A woman she had never seen before knelt, her face inches from Merrilee's. "Your arms are scraped; is your thumb out of joint?" she said, half-lifting Merrilee by the elbows to a sitting position. "Your knee looks raw; that's got to hurt."

"I'm all right, just a klutz," Merrilee answered and shook her head again. "I need to get to the wifi, make a phone call." White girl, she thought, curly brown hair. In the center of one yellow-gray eye the pupil glinted, a spark in a stormy autumn night sky that then disappeared, a falling star. "Right away," she added.

"Merrilee, where's your dad? What happened?" asked Theresa.

On her feet, Merrilee called to her mother as she hurried, favoring one knee, into the visitor center, the woman with the sparkly pupil at her side. "Dad's fine, Mom—he's back by the hill. We went in past the trail, and there's been some kind of rockslide at the settlement, and he wants me to tell Scott, and to call Jack to come look at it. We need to get people off the trail; he says it might be dangerous."

Her daughter's eyes were bright: her world had changed, but in a way that Theresa, in her concern for Michael, didn't notice yet nevertheless felt, as Merrilee and the woman visitor with the starlit eye walked toward the visitor center.

In the ranger's office, Scott Martin listened as Merrilee called Jack Minogeezhik, the Mozhay Point tribal chairman. "I'm at Miskwaa; the ranger's here with me, and there's a problem. I came here with Michael to look at the lumber road. You know he was doing that today? There's something going on here that he thinks you want to come look at, a rockslide at Odanang; he wants to know could you get here pretty soon . . . He told me to get people off the hiking trail and back to the visitor center but not say anything until you get here . . . I'll tell him. See ya."

"I'll tell the staff that there's a problem out on the trails," said Scott. "And they can watch things here while we get people off them by the hill and direct them to the riverwalk or back to the parking lot and visitor center. Is the girl out by the desk there with you? Can she help?"

"I just met her, but sure, she'll help."

"If people ask, tell them that there's been a minor washout on the trail and the park ranger is just going out to make sure it is safe. Tell them again, if they ask, that the riverwalk is open."

Margie, Theresa, and the woman with the sparkly eye were waiting outside for Merrilee.

"So tell us what happened," said Theresa. "What was your dad doing poking around the settlement?"

"Well," began Merrilee, "he said he wanted to look at the lumber road from the top of the hill, so when we got to that sign that says No Entry-Danger-Unstable Rocks, you know, at the split in the trail where people used to go from the inlet to the settlement? We went in and were going to go around to the other side of the hill, because the settlement side is so eroded; well, it looks like part of the hill slid down, isn't there anymore, so we went closer—"

"You went closer? You could have gotten hurt!" said Theresa.

"—and the hill had chunked off and took a lot of other rocks and some little trees and brush with it, and everything rolled all the way down onto the back of the Etienne store—part of it caved in and the rest is covered, pretty much. And Dad thinks that Jack needs to see it. He wants me to get people off the path, have them come back here. I think he is worried that more of the hill could cave in, maybe reach the trail. Do you want to help? We can take the ranger bikes, you go north on the path and I'll go south." This to the sparkly-eyed woman.

"Sure—what about your thumb?"

"My thumb?" Merrilee looked at it. "Oh, it always pops in and out like that; it's fine. My name's Merrilee; you've probably already heard that."

"Ann. Pleased to meet you." The pupil in her left eye flashed, a split second of brilliant silver.

The Mozhay Point economic development committee was responding favorably to the Wing Development consultant's presentation, and tribal chair Jack Minogeezhik nodded at the young woman who was wrapping up her PowerPoint with small nervous glances at the row of Wing Developoment representatives at the side of the room:

"To return to the key points of Mozhay Point recreation center," she said, "let's revisit the slides":

♦ The Mozhay Point Band of Ojibwe is in good fiscal position to develop a year-round indoor-outdoor recreation area in a partnership with the Minnesota state parks system.

◆ As you can see on the map, the Band owns six forty-
acre parcels of land at the northwest corner of the reservation that are not assigned to individuals under the
land allotments of the late nineteenth and early twenti-
eth centuries. This abuts the Miskwaa River State Park;
you can see on the map that the reservation boundaries
are not far from the river; the park is not that large.

◆ The Miskwaa River State Park has seen an increase in
use as interest in outdoor activities by off-reservation
populations has risen. This has created a strain on the
facilities and, more important, the natural resources of
the area.

◆ A visitor center, built by the State of Minnesota and
run by the Mozhay Point Band members as a cooperative endeavor, is in need of repair and expansion. Both
Mozhay Point and the State of Minnesota have indi-
cated a desire to improve the site and offerings.

◆ Visitors to Miskwaa River Park access it by way of
County Road 5, which bisects Highway 53 at the town
of Mesabi, thirty miles to the east. The Mozhay Point
tribal offices and school are located midway between
Mesabi and the Miskwaa River State Park. West of the
tribal offices the road, which was never built for heavy
visitor use to the park, is in disrepair.

◆ On the north side of the Miskwaa River visitor center,
a series of abandoned lumber company roads intersect
and connect in what can be seen from above as a nearly
straight line to the north side of Mesabi. One of these
roads, the Tweten, is situated within a mile of the tribal
office buildings.

◆ The State of Minnesota is willing to assume the cost
of rebuilding the lumber road as well as expanding the

visitor center. The combined and interconnected locations of the Miskwaa River Park and the Mozhay Point year-round recreation center will be a groundbreaking historic cooperative agreement between two governments, tribal and state.

"This concludes our slide presentation, the beginning of what we anticipate will be a productive win-win partnership between the Mozhay Point Band and Wing Development. We certainly thank the development committee for reviewing this, our initial proposal. We thank you for your invitation to propose, and we of course want to have all our ducks in a row for the tribal council meeting, if the development committee project is approved by the tribal council. Does anyone have any questions?"

Tammy Ricebird raised a hand. "I can see on the map that just before you get to those four big allotments that Mozhay owns, those old roads curve away from one part of the reservation—that would be the LaForce allotment, right?"

"Committee Chair Dommage, would you like to speak to that?" asked the young woman.

"Ye-e-s, what you see is right, Tammy," answered Jason Dommage. "That is where the new road would have to be cut, otherwise we'd have the same problems in that area as we do now, on the road to Sweetgrass and the river. The tribal council will make a decision on offering a deal for the LaForce allotment; as you know, this is nothing new: many tribes have land buyback programs."

"Isn't that close to their sugar bush?"

One of the row of Wing men at the back of the room rose. "Chair Dommage, I believe I can answer that question. Our environmental experts, working with Mozhay Point and the state, will ensure minimal impact, if any, on the natural resources of the area."

Tammy was becoming annoyed. "Can you just *go ahead* and buy an allotment? What if the stakeholders don't want to sell? Has anybody asked Margie Robineau? She's the one who lives there; why isn't she at this meeting?"

"This is all very preliminary at this point," said Jack. "We're here to listen today, and this committee will review and make a recommendation to the council." He put a hand over his jacket pocket, where his cell phone buzzed and vibrated. "The council is aware of this; we have hired Wing Development to do this preliminary look at the feasibility of the project."

"So I am asking again: why isn't Margie Robineau invited to this meeting to speak for her family, the Gallettes and LaForces?" asked Tammy. "And the Council of Elders—aren't you thinking of asking them?"

"Tammy . . . ," began Jason Dommage. "Look, I get that I'm new to development, but I know what our job is, which is to study and recommend, and the council makes the final decisions. I apologize, Tammy; I don't mean to correct you, but we have to follow policies set by the tribe."

Jack's phone chimed; he looked into his pocket and turned it upright. The text was from Merrilee Washington: *Pls call. Urgent.*

"I'm sorry, but I'm going to have to leave. Do you need me for anything else?"

"We're good here, Chief. Migwech for your time," said Jason. "We'll take a ten-minute break here and then meet in the Biindigen Room for lunch. Please order anything you like from the menu; the feature today is the Lost Lake duck confit."

*

His meeting with the tribal economic development committee interrupted, Jack Minogeezhik drove his Escalade only slightly faster than the posted 20 mph speed limit along the curves and dips on the road from Sweetgrass, the SUV bouncing and spitting gravel even at this speed. His wife, Dale Ann, the Mozhay Point director of education, sat in the passenger seat; after listening from the hallway to the telephone call from Merrilee about the rockslide at Half-Dime Hill, she had grabbed her windbreaker and extra pair of tennis shoes from the closet and followed Jack outside to the parking lot. Jack started the Escalade, told Dale Ann to put on her seat belt, and drove diagonally over the parking spaces painted on the blacktop, over the grass boulevard and gravel shoulder onto the road to Sweetgrass and the state park.

"Nobody is hurt, that you know?" asked Dale Ann.

"As far as Merrilee knew; unless some jerk ignored the signs and left the trails. Gawd. It's just lucky that Michael was already out there when it happened."

"I would have been there for coffee with Margie and Theresa, but I decided I should go into the office instead." Dale Ann was semiretired.

"See what you're missing out on? When are you going to retire for good?"

"I know I should; somebody else would love a crack at this job. I'm thinking in two years, when your term is up. Nobody knows you're not running again, right? Two years out like that, anything can happen in the meantime that you'd change your mind."

"Nope; Michael sounded like he was fishing around after the last council meeting. So far as I can tell, he's going to run for council again this spring, but I think it will be it;

he'll serve out his last four-year term and retire. If he gets reelected."

"Well, that could all change if he finds you're not going to run next time. And if he doesn't get elected this time, that will be an early end to you guys tag-teaming on the council!" Dale Ann laughed. "What a pair, is all I can say."

Jack squeezed her elbow. "The Miskwaa project will be the last big thing, lay the groundwork for years to come—no, decades. God, lucky the slide was on the settlement side of Half-Dime; if it was on the lumber road side, we might have to kiss any hope for a cell tower anytime soon goodbye, and that is something we really need."

"I don't know the last time I was on the settlement side of the hill," Dale Ann said and then was silent.

At Sweetgrass, the LaForce allotment land, they passed Beryl Duhlebon's bright-pink mailbox, then Margie Robineau's fire number marker painted on a post at the end of her sumac-choked driveway. "No matter what Margie is thinking, the project will happen: the council has a good idea of what Development will recommend and will approve most of it. No way she is going to be able to do the whole thing in. Between the elections this year, the road, the park improvements . . . It will all turn out to be lot of fuss and some wasted money and time, and she'll end up getting her heart broken over a piece of land that will end belonging to the tribe, as it was before Mozhay was divided up into individual allotments. Are you hearing anything from her about it?"

"Not really—nothing new anyway." Dale Ann knew that if she repeated everything Margie said to her to her husband, the tribal chair, that source of information would soon dry up.

Past the boat landing on Lost Lake, the road appeared to end after a tight curve and parking area. Practiced, Jack slowed for the hairpin curve. The Escalade growled onto the stretch of straight road that followed, dust rising in its wake.

Dale Ann kept a grip on both arm rests. "She doesn't talk about it to me; maybe to Theresa. Why don't you ask Michael?"

"Anything I already know about Margie is what I get from Michael."

"Park sign coming up, just one more minute," Jack muttered, then he heard a siren and red lights flashed in the rearview mirror.

"What the hell?!" Jack pulled off the road and stopped. "Tribal police?"

The vehicle, a van with Mozhay Emergency Medical & Rescue painted on the side, passed the truck; the driver glanced at Dale Ann.

"Oh, my god, it's Dag," breathed Dale Ann. "Was somebody hurt after all?"

The rear wheels on the Escalade spun and the vehicle fishtailed as Jack accelerated, as if on an icy winter patch, then gripped the road, and followed the ambulance.

At the visitor center, Joey and Miigwan were nervously serving free soft drinks from the concession stand window to everyone gathered in the parking lot, who craned their necks all in the same direction looking up at the two elderly hikers clinging to a small tree on the side of Half-Dime Hill. Margie and Theresa, who had declined the free drinks, were waiting at the Jeep, Theresa in the passenger seat with the door open, and Margie leaning against the hood. Merrilee and Ann waited at the entrance to the trails with Michael and the park ranger, who signaled the ambulance to stop at the hiking trail entrance.

The two EMTs, Dag Bjornborg and Tyler Ricebird, opened the back of the ambulance as they spoke with Jack, who had parked next to the visitor center building and rushed over to the ambulance. Margie and Theresa immediately start talking with Dale Ann about how the couple must have ignored the warning signs and tried to hike up the hill, and then Margie thought she saw something reflecting the sun, and it was them, the hikers stuck up on the side of the hill calling for help. They watched Michael talking with the EMTs and pointing to the side of the hill, the hikers waving, and the EMTs unloading equipment from the back of the ambulance and carrying it on a gurney to the trailhead. Michael and Jack remained at the ambulance, talking quietly and, as it looked to Margie, Dale Ann, and Theresa, urgently.

Dag returned to the trail entrance. "They look like they're all right, but we're not going to be able to get them down from here. Tyler is talking with them, trying to calm them down. They picked the worse part of the hill to try to climb. Things are really loose and they didn't bother with the sign that said so. The man keeps talking about an urn he dropped, and the woman is afraid that they are both going to slide down the hill after it—and that's honestly going to happen if the guy doesn't settle down. What we're going to do is go up from the back side of the hill and go down from the top to pull them up."

"Are you going to need more people, equipment?" asked Scott.

"We might; come with us to see what you think, okay? And can you get somebody to keep people away from the hill, both sides? Clear the trails?"

"We got people off the trails that we could see easily." Merrilee and Ann had been edging closer and closer as Jack and Michael were talking. "But, yeah, we'll go look for anybody else."

"Tell them they can have a free pop at the visitor center if they want—the kids working there know that—and if anybody wants to hike they can go down by the inlet and the river but no place else." Jack paused. "And don't leave. We might need you."

"Chief, why don't you come with, to take a look at where that guy's silver chalice, or whatever that thing is, landed; it's on the shed in back of the Etienne house. I think we can get it for him, but there's some damage you'll want to see," said Michael to Jack.

The dull ping of the rock against the man's hat had been a satisfying sound to Therese LaForce, who with Beryl, Rose, and Artense had been watching the hikers from the half-circle of their webbed lawn chairs at the top of Half-Dime Hill. She nodded approvingly at her daughter-in-law. "Artense, I will admit that you are a better shot than I am."

"You got things started, my girl, good for you," said Beryl.

"And on her first try, too. Wuh," added Rose.

Pleased, Artense blushed. The ladies: Therese perched on the edge of her lawn chair smoking her clay pipe; Rose, easing the waistband of her polyester pants as she settled into her chair; and Beryl, hands resting regally on the arms of her chair and her elaborate updo a queenly crown. They quieted as they watched the destiny of Sweetgrass play out, assisted by a skillfully aimed rock.

The two men, one heavy above the waist and one heavy all over, walked into the brush, following a path no longer visible to the eye but indelibly recorded into their memories by the ancestors, and toward the Odanang settlement.

part ii.
mewinzhaa, 1972

the dionne fork

ON AN EARLY AUTUMN DAY not long after the end of that
year's Mozhay Point ricing season, a blue 1961 Ford truck
with a tan 1963 tailgate pulled up at the gas pump in front of
the Skelly station where it braked hard, the driver clearly in
a hurry. Jumping out the door, he grabbed the nozzle on the
gas pump, calling toward the garage, "Eugene! On my way
to work—I'll pay inside!"

"Boozhoo, Michael!" the voice was muffled. "Go ahead,
Niijii."

Michael Washington pumped two dollars' worth of gas
into the truck and took the wooden stairs into the store two
at a time. Inside, he handed two bills to the old man sitting
behind the counter. "I got gas."

"You got time to visit?" Mr. Tuomela was always happy
for business—and company.

"Going to be late for work," Michael explained, his hand
on the doorknob.

"At the camp? When does it close?"

"Another month yet. The kids' sessions are done, but
they're going to have some overnight sessions for adults—
church groups, mostly." Michael's job as custodian at a camp
north of Mesabi was seasonal. "They don't like it when I
don't get there on time. See you later, and say hello to Mrs.

Tuomela for me!" Michael ran down the steps two at a time, started the truck, and headed toward Mesabi.

The toilet in the half-bath next to the entryway flushed. "Say, Dale Ann, you just missed Michael," Mr. Tuomela called toward the bathroom door. Water running from the faucet, the girl inside didn't hear and didn't answer. He raised his voice toward the back of the store. "Helmi, remind me to tell Dale Ann that Michael Washington was here."

Dale Ann Dionne, who had spent the past hour cleaning the fixtures and floor in the small bathroom closet at the front of the Tuomelas' Skelly station and store, was washing her hands, turning the bar of Dial soap over and over in her wet palms, and then rinsing the lather down the sink drain. She dried her hands on the clean towel she had hung on the bar attached to the sink and pushed up her glasses, which had slipped halfway down her nose.

"Bathroom's done," she called toward the living quarters at the back of the store. "Anything else you want me to do? It's almost eleven o'clock; bus should be here anytime. I can get the mail bag."

"Watch for it, will you, Dale Ann? I'm frying some bologna for sandwiches. And potatoes."

The smell of cut and frying onions, the second ingredient after the lump of lard that Mrs. Tuomela placed in the frying pan for most things she cooked, hung in the air over the kitchen, bedroom, and storefront. Mrs. Tuomela cooked fried bologna sandwiches and potatoes for lunch, the biggest meal of their day, three or four days a week. On the other days she usually boiled the potatoes while frying the hamburger into small loose pieces, to which she added flour and milk to make a gravy, then poured the mixture over the potatoes. Mr. Tuomela never seemed to notice the limited

menu of the midday lunch, called dinner at the Dionne Fork
and throughout Mozhay Point, as well as across most of the
Iron Range of Minnesota.

"Dinner almost ready?" Mr. Tuomela breathed in the
fumes and sighed in appreciation. "Smells like the Ritz."

Eugene Dionne, Dale Ann's cousin, was the general
handyman for the gas station and store who worked on cars
in the garage and was the delivery driver for the Tuomelas'
contracted star mail delivery route. Like Mr. Tuomela, he
never seemed to tire of the menu and made similar comments before the midday meal every day. Although dinner
was part of his pay, he invariably acted the role of guest,
happily surprised at the menu, expressing his appreciation for Mrs. Tuomela's cooking before and while he ate,
and always announcing after that he was *so* full. Dale Ann
expected that today would be the same, Mrs. Tuomela asking if Eugene was sure he had had enough, and wondering
where a skinny fellow like him put it all. Mr. Tuomela would
declare to Mother (his wife) that a hardworking young man
like Eugene, *he just works it all off,* and then heave himself
up from his chair and thump with his crutch to the counter
at the front of the store to work on his crossword puzzle and
watch the road.

"You'll have some dinner with us, won't you, Dale Ann?"

"Sure, thanks; I'd love some." Because she liked Mrs.
Tuomela so much, it would take years, even decades, for
Dale Ann to realize and admit to herself how much she disliked onions. "Anything else you want me to do? Help you
fry the potatoes?"

"No, sweetheart, I don't need anything. You take a
break, get off your feet."

"Why don't she sit out on the stairs to watch for the bus,

get herself some fresh air," suggested Mr. Tuomela from the counter. "I'll sit with you, Dale Ann; could use some air and some sun myself." He bobbed two steps on one leg to the top of the basement stairs, where he lifted a wooden crutch from its hook, then step-hopped to the front door. His threadbare Dickey's work shirt and pants, put on clean that morning, were pinned neatly, one pants leg to above the knee and one shirtsleeve to the opposite shoulder; shirt and pants bore stiff creases and shine from Mrs. Tuomela's iron pressed heavily onto Argo-soaked cotton. From habit, Dale Ann knew not to offer assistance as the old man swung his body from the railing two steps from the top of the stairs and settled himself on the comfortable give of soft wooden stairs. He leaned back against the railing on one side of the stairway, Dale Ann on the other.

"Pretty day," he commented. "Smells like fall, like it's not too long till snow. And look at that blue sky." He began to sing his favorite song, "Blue Skirt Waltz," his aging vocal cords cracking on the higher notes and rumbling on the lower. The old man and girl watched as two cars passed, one headed east toward Mesabi and the highway, and one heading west from Mesabi toward Sweetgrass. Each honked, the driver and passengers waving and Dale Ann and Mr. Tuomela waving back.

"Blue were the skies, blue were your eyes," sang Mr. Tuomela. Across the road Dale Ann's mother, Grace, peered out the front room window of the Dionne house, also looking for the bus, which would bring the mail, and came out the front door onto the stoop where she craned her neck to see around the curve of County Road 5. Grace had changed out her usual white cotton dish towel that she wore turban-style over her pincurls to her red nylon chiffon, too bright for church in her view but her favorite color, and good for going out of the house.

Mr. Tuomela finished his song: "Come back, blue lady, come back, and don't be blue anymore," before raising his voice to carry across the road. "Bus ain't here yet!"

From the side of the Dionne house a cat emerged from the long grass waving in the breeze from the rarely used and barely visible Kangas Road next to the Dionne outhouse and butted its head against the front door. In the cat's mouth was half a field mouse, an offering that he laid at Grace's feet. Limber and stringy, she rested one hand lightly on the doorknob as if it were a barre; ballerina-like she kicked the tiny carcass off the stoop, then pivoted on her other foot to nudge the cat inside the house.

"My baby girl Cecile is taking me to Mesabi to go to the Pamida," she called back, "but I want to see if we got anything in the mail first." She began to sweep the stairs, her face turned toward the bus as if willing it to appear.

"Dinner's ready two minutes!" Mrs. Tuomela called from the kitchen. "Jorma, come help set the table; Dale Ann, go tell Eugene it's time to eat!"

"Be there in two shakes of a lamb's tail, blue skirt girl!" The old man grabbed the stairway railing, lifting himself to one foot. Hopping one step up to the top he swung his arm over the crutch and thumped into the store.

Mrs. Tuomela watched Dale Ann from the storefront window, thinking that the girl walked so slowly and heavily for someone so young. Like she's got the world on her shoulders, she said to herself. In the kitchen, she set four plates on the table. "She's still so quiet, Jorma; don't you think so?"

"She always was a quiet girl, Mother; still is. Still waters

run deep. Nice to have around the place, I always think."
Mr. Tuomela carried four coffee cups one at a time in four
trips, lifting them from the hooks they hung on below the
dish cupboard with his single arm and maneuvering a finger through each handle, then placing each to the right of
a plate.

"But different from when she was a child. She never said
much when she came back from Chicago, and since she
came back from Duluth last year she—I don't know, she
looks like she's got something heavy on her mind."

"She's growing up. One of these days she'll get herself
a job someplace else and leave us, and it'll really be quiet
around here then. You'll miss her, won't you, Helmi?"

Mrs. Tuomela sighed. "The way she wraps her arms
across her waist like that, I wonder if something is hurting
her. She seems healthy enough, I suppose, but so sad and
lost. She could use somebody to take care of her."

"Well, then, she could get married. She could stay here
and she could marry Eugene; he's a good, steady boy; the
kind that works on cars always is."

"They're cousins, Jorma—my goodness, what a thought.
Not first cousins, but they are cousins, just the same."

"The two of them, we could sell them the store someday.
Or maybe the reservation would buy it and hire the kids:
Dale Ann could run the store, and Eugene could run the
gas station and the garage. They could get married and start
a nice little family. And we could move into one of those
senior citizen apartments in Mesabi."

"You are such a daydreamer." Helmi imagined a small
child, Dale Ann and Eugene's little one asking her, Mumu,
for a cookie, a glass of milk. "But I don't think she's going to
marry Eugene, or anybody else. Her mother says she is so

religious, took that vow that she would never get married; not that I believe much of what Grace ever says." She pictured Grace scolding the little one, Grace's own grandchild, to be quiet and stop running around on her clean floor. What kind of grandmother would that crab ever make, anyway?

"Well, then, if she doesn't get married, maybe she'll go back to that convent in Duluth. Smart girl like Dale Ann, she'd be a crackerjack nun."

The convent. Mrs. Tuomela clicked her tongue and sighed.

In the garage, Eugene was talking softly, as was his habit, to a spark plug, holding it up to the light. "I don't see a crack there at all; think you want to give it one more try?" he asked, lifting his thick-lensed, black-framed glasses above his eyes and to his forehead. He squinted. "Once more, to make sure."

Although Eugene's and Dale Ann's fathers were first cousins, there wasn't much physical resemblance between their children except for their thick, shiny hair, their near-sighted, almond-shaped eyes, and their identical heavy-lensed, black-framed Indian Health Service–issued glasses. Eugene's glasses fit tightly against the sides of his head, denting the shape of his Brylcreemed hair, combed to resemble Elvis Presley's. Dale Ann's glasses slipped—endlessly and annoyingly—from the small bump at the top of her long nose and were constantly being pushed up by her middle finger.

"Eugene, Mrs. Tuomela says dinner's ready." Dale Ann pushed up her glasses.

Eugene lay the spark plug on a crate he had nailed into

the wall as a shelf. "Dinnertime already? You gonna eat here, too?"

"Yeah, I'm going to stay and watch the store while Mr. Tuomela takes his nap. Mrs. Tuomela wants to go on the mail route with you; Beryl Duhlebon has a grocery order and she wants to trade for some wild rice."

Eugene stopped at the side of the store building to turn on the water spigot and rinse his hands. Dale Ann said the words she always said: "You can wash inside."

Eugene replied with the words he always said: "I want to get as much dirt off as I can before I use the sink; keep the bathroom clean." He rubbed his hands together under the cold water, scrubbed at the backs and between his fingers, and inspected his nails. Drying his hands on the shop towel tucked into his belt, he said, "Wait a minute before we go in, Dale Ann. I wanted to tell you that I applied for a job in Mesabi: full-time mechanic at the Conoco garage."

"Really?" She had never thought that Eugene would leave the gas station.

"They offered it to me, and I'm going to take it. Don't say anything to Mr. and Mrs. Tuomela, okay?"

"Well, that's terrific, Eugene! Mr. and Mrs. Tuomela will miss you, no doubt about that! And I won't say anything. When do you start?"

"Two weeks from next Monday. I told them I'd give Mr. and Mrs. Tuomela two weeks' notice. I've got to tell them today or tomorrow. They've been good to me; I really hate to leave them, but I've got to think about the future. Conoco is a company: they pay decent, I'll get raises, and insurance, and the experience—they'll train me to do things

I don't know. Who knows, maybe I'll even be part owner someday."

"You'd be a businessman!"

"Maybe I'm getting ahead of myself, but it's been my dream, a good job and not having to leave Mozhay." Eugene straightened the towel and smoothed it, cleared his throat. "Or at least not go far away from home." He cleared his throat again. "I might be moving to Mesabi. I met a girl, and if I lived in town, I'd be able to see her more."

"Wow, Eugene—what's her name? Is she one of the girls from school?"

"Naw, she's from Embarrass; her family has a farm. Her name is Fern, Fern Lampi. She works at the Ben Franklin store in Mesabi. I met her at the movies; she was there with her roommate. She's . . . well, she's a real nice girl." He blushed.

Dale Ann wondered if Fern Lampi was the cashier at the Ben Franklin so bashful that she ducked her head when she said, "Thank you," her untidy red hair hanging into her face as she barely got the words out. How in the world had Eugene managed to get her to talk with him? "She must be nice if you like her. I'm really happy for you."

"Once I get things settled, I am going to bring her by the house to see everybody."

"That's great." Dale Ann's smile was beginning to feel forced.

"I was wondering if you would want to go into Mesabi with me sometime, maybe next weekend. You could meet Fern; maybe we'd go to a movie."

"That'd be nice." Was she clenching her teeth as she grinned like a jack-o'-lantern? "Well, guess we should go in to dinner." The creases at the corners of Dale Ann's eyes felt sore above her stiff cheeks. "It'll be a celebration dinner, except the Tuomelas won't know."

Eugene wondered when had been the last time he had seen Dale Ann in good spirits. What had gone wrong for her when she went to Chicago to work as a telephone operator and returned to Mozhay, and then left for the convent in Duluth to become a religious sister? How did she feel returning home twice like that, after her mother had bragged to everybody about her great job, then about Father Hagen picking her to go to the convent in Duluth to learn to be a nun? He paused at the bottom stairs and asked, "Do you have a dream job, little cousin, something you especially would like to do? I mean, you know, if you could do whatever you wanted, anything?"

And as they walked through the doorway into the store, Dale Ann told Eugene what she had never told anyone else. "If I could do anything I wanted, I would go to college, and I'd be a teacher."

Mrs. Tuomela waved Dale Ann and Eugene to chairs at the table. "Sit down; eat it while it's hot," she said, thinking to herself, *I wonder what those two were talking about out there; they both look like butter wouldn't melt in their mouths. Maybe Jorma is onto something, maybe they are sweet on each, after all.*

Dale Ann watched the scene inside the Tuomela kitchen unfold as if it were an overly rehearsed play, and she and Eugene actors who knew everyone's lines by heart:

Scene: The Tuomela Gas and Grocery kitchen. Yellow walls, one window with flowered curtains above a sink, dish rag draped over faucet. Table covered with oilcloth. Four mismatched chairs. Stove and refrigerator of any model, dish towel draped over oven door handle and refrigerator door handle. Fry pan, tea kettle, and coffee-pot on top of the stove. Mismatched dishes and utensils on table, ketchup and mustard bottles, salt and pepper shakers. Mr. Tuomela is seated at the table. Mrs. Tuomela stands in front of the stove.

Dale Ann does not speak. Sits with arms crossed over waist and pressed against her middle during the entire scene. She will nod at Mrs. Tuomela's comments, direct her attention without expression toward Eugene when he speaks, smile at Mr. Tuomela's humorous lines.

EUGENE: Fried bologna sandwiches! Man, I could smell them out in the garage!

MR. TUOMELA: How's Pearl Minogeezhik's car sounding?

EUGENE: Purring like a kitten when I get done with it. These are the most delicious fried potatoes I ever ate!

MRS. TUOMELA: Pearl, she'll pay cash, I betcha; she always pays cash, never asks for credit.

MR. TUOMELA: Mother, can you reach the coffeepot?

MRS. TUOMELA: If you want to go with Grace and Cecile to the Pamida, Dale Ann, I don't need to go to Beryl's today. Want another sandwich, Eugene?

EUGENE: I already ate two; best bologna sandwiches on Mozhay Point! Are there any more potatoes?

MRS. TUOMELA: I don't know where he puts it all.

MR. TUOMELA: Young guy like Eugene, keeps busy, he works it off. Or maybe he's got a hollow leg!

Eugene, Mr. Tuomela, and Mrs. Tuomela laugh.

> Dale Ann sits with arms crossed over waist and pressed against her middle during the entire scene, does not speak. Nods at Mrs. Tuomela's comments, smiles at Eugene's comments, laughs at Mr. Tuomela's jokes.

> A horn honks twice from offstage.

> EUGENE: The bus. I'll get it!

> Rises from his chair and exits stage left.

> Stage lights dim to darkness.

In early spring of her senior year at Mesabi High School, not long after the maple sugar harvest, Dale Ann had been pulled out of English, her favorite class, to meet with a recruiter from the federal government's Federal Relocation Program. The recruiter, Mr. Gunderson, was boyish and earnest; his dark hair curled stylishly over his collar, and he was impressed with Dale Ann's grades and her attitude. She had been recommended by her teachers and was exactly the kind of young person the program was looking for, he told her. The relocation program was offering her training and a job as a telephone operator in Chicago, Illinois: she would not only learn a skill that would make her employable in good-paying work for the rest of her life; why, some telephone operators even became secretaries in major corporations. When Dale Ann hesitatingly mentioned the possibility of working in an office for one of the mining companies, Mr. Gunderson pointed out the lack of opportunities for an American Indian girl in northern Minnesota, even ones with good grades who could type. He turned from flirtatiously earnest to bare-bones no-nonsense: "There's no future up here for a girl like you. Do you want to waitress, work at a resort? You could do that, but do you really see that for yourself? Life here can be hard, Dale Ann.

It can be a hard life here for a girl like you, a girl with your kind of potential. This is the way out, Dale Ann, but it's up to you. The decision is yours."

Her mother, Grace, told Dale Ann that this was the opportunity of a lifetime.

By the end of the school year the relocation worker on the Chicago end, Miss Novak, had taken care of everything and added her own touches. Miss Novak thought that Chicago was perhaps too big-city for Dale Ann, that Dale Ann would be more successful in Evanston, the small city on the northern edge of Chicago, and that she would like living with other girls her own age. Miss Novak visited her own college, Northwestern, from which she had graduated only a few years earlier, and found a flyer on a bulletin board in Scott Hall, the student union, that two sophomores were looking for a third girl beginning fall quarter. With Miss Novak's guarantee of the rent being paid on time, the students agreed, one enthusiastically and the other agreeably.

After Labor Day, Dale Ann took the Greyhound to Chicago, where she was met at the bus station by Miss Novak, who had a great smile and, she said, just *loved* her job helping young American Indian people from reservations get off to a great start in life. She solicitously settled Dale Ann, her new suitcase, and a large plastic shopping bag in her car, a gold Camaro ("From my parents for graduation—isn't it adorable?").

During the drive to Evanston, Miss Novak asked Dale Ann about her family, school, her friends, and life at Mozhay Point. Did she have a boyfriend, Miss Novak wanted to know, hoping that she didn't—a boyfriend at home boded ill for any success for relocation girls.

"No; I mean, I have a friend who is a boy, but he's not my boyfriend. He's in the Army. In Viet Nam."

The Army? Miss Novak looked embarrassed for Dale Ann and her friend who was in the Army and changed the subject. "You will love what the girls have done with the apartment, and with your room. I took the liberty of buying sheets and blankets so you wouldn't have so much to do when you arrived."

Elizabeth and Catherine ("Everyone calls us Buff and Cat") were waiting with the door to the apartment open— Catherine thin and hatchet-faced, with shiny eyes and a never-fading smile, and Elizabeth, dark-haired and rather beautiful as well as somewhat suspicious and watchful. Like her mother, thought Dale Ann. They had set the table in the dining alcove with hot chocolate, tea, and a box of assorted Dunkin' Donuts and chattered with Miss Novak as though she was a school friend, referencing buildings and professors that she remembered, laughing and saying, "Oh, yes!"

Remembering Dale Ann, who was silently nibbling on a frosted donut, unable to think of anything to say, Miss Novak brought the conversation with the college girls back to their new roommate. Elizabeth was reserved, responding politely, "Of course," to questions about their willingness to introduce and acclimate Dale Ann to her new life. Catherine, however, sparkled and chattered about Friday afternoons on Deering Meadow, concerts and programs at Scott Hall, and the many friends they would introduce the shy new girl to. "And we hope you will come visit us," she said to the relocation worker. "We would love to see you!"

Miss Novak thought it had been a super afternoon and said so. As she left she said, "Now, you will call me, won't you, if you need anything or have any questions, anything at all, right?"

"What nice girls," she thought to herself. "This will be so much more fun for Dale Ann than living by herself in some dreary room in downtown Chicago. And she can walk to Illinois Bell from the apartment."

"Well! We didn't even get the chance to show you your room," said Cat. She opened a door off the living room. "Ta-daa! What do you think?"

The room, which had been intended as a study, had a window in the top half of the door and two outside windows that looked onto a vacant lot with a single young tree. The girls had, as Cat had written, made up the bed with the new floral sheets and pastel blankets purchased by Miss Novak. Cat had leaned a baby doll and a Raggedy Ann back against the pillows and had tacked a floral pillowcase over the top half of the door. "It looks like you have another window to the outside, doesn't it?"

Dale Ann, who had never had a room to herself, would have liked to go inside and close the door; instead, she sat on the bed and said, "It is so pretty." Buff placed Dale Ann's plastic bag on the wooden chair next to the bed, and the new suitcase, which she seemed to find distasteful, on the floor. "We'll let you get settled," she said. She and Cat left, closing the door.

And Dale Ann was alone, in her own room, the overhead light in the living room an incandescent sun illuminating the roses and daisies in the pillowcase that covered the window to the living room.

*

"The bus is here! Mail time!" His face turned to the front window, Mr. Tuomela sounded surprised and excited, as he did every time the Greyhound pulled up next to the gas pump.

"I'll get it!" Eugene bounded down the stairs and over to the baggage compartment at the side of the bus, where the driver was pushing suitcases aside. "Hi, Norman."

"Hello, Eugene. Nobody for the bus today? I've got eight passengers to pick up in Mesabi, most going all the way to the Falls."

"Nobody today."

"Do you know if Jorma sold any tickets for this coming week, to Duluth or to the Falls? Or to Mesabi?" Norman pulled a canvas sack from between a footlocker and a suitcase. "*Here* it is."

"Not so far." Mrs. Tuomela was standing in the doorway. "You know how it is here: most people don't buy their ticket ahead of time, just show up at the store."

Norman handed the canvas U.S. Mail sack to Eugene. "I keep hearing that one of these days the HCR contractors are going to have to go to Mesabi for the mail drop. Greyhound's losing money because of not enough passengers, not enough going in and out of the Dionne Fork stop. Got to sell some tickets to keep this going."

Eugene nodded politely; Mrs. Tuomela said, "We'll do what we can."

Back in the store, Mr. Tuomela spread the mail out on the counter with his single hand, sorting according to route numbers with a delight that never flagged from day to day. The most pieces were for the Mozhay Point tribal building; the rest—letters, bills, advertisements, and an occasional magazine—would go to the scattered addresses on the route.

"Lot of ads today, coupons from the IGA, and political ads. Just about everybody will get mail," he said happily. "Line 'em up in the box, will you, Eugene?"

"Dale Ann, your mother wants the mail before she goes to Mesabi; walk it over there, will you, before we leave on the route," said Mrs. Tuomela. "Looks like a bill, and coupons."

"Well, will you look at this—Dale Ann, there's a letter for you!" HCR Contractor Tuomela could hardly contain his excitement. "A little pink envelope from Chicago—one of your girlfriends there sent you a card! It's not your birthday yet, she's a little early." He pushed the envelope to the edge of the counter.

Dale Ann tucked the envelope into her sweater pocket and crossed the road to bring the rest of the Dionne household mail to Grace, who was already waiting in the car with Cecile.

"Sure you don't want to come with?" Cecile wrinkled her nose, mouthed, "Come on—pleeease."

Dale Ann pinched the pink envelope between finger and thumb, pressing it into the corner of her sweater pocket. "Got to watch the store," she answered, her hand curling the small pink envelope into a *u*-shape in her pocket. "See you when you get back."

Cecile stuck out her tongue and rolled up the car window.

In the driveway, Eugene was securing the cardboard box of mail in the back seat of his black '57 Buick, bought from Father Hagen when he replaced it with a newer and also black model. He opened the passenger door for Mrs. Tuomela, who half-rolled onto the seat and pulled her housedress down over her knees modestly, settling the box of groceries for Beryl Duhlebon on her lap.

"Hamburger, instant coffee, can of beans, eggs, milk—five things," Mrs. Tuomela counted on her fingers. "I think that's everything she said. You'll carry the box in for me, won't you, and I'll visit with Beryl and see what she wants for their wild rice. You can pick me up after you finish the end of the route. Dale Ann, wake Jorma up at 2:00 or so if he doesn't get up by himself?"

The Buick didn't so much purr as growl gently as Eugene drove west on the road toward Sweetgrass. I can't believe Father Hagen would let this car out of his hands, he thought as he adjusted the air vents. "That blowing too hard on you?" he asked Mrs. Tuomela.

In the kitchen, Dale Ann felt the pink envelope in her sweater pocket, her fingers gripping it into a cylinder. Suddenly powerfully thirsty, she poured a glass of water and drank it all without stopping, then rinsed the glass and wiped it with a dish towel, turning it in the light from the window over the sink to inspect it for smears. She squinted, rinsed, and wiped it again and looked out the window at the backyard, where the Tuomelas' laundry waved in the breeze. She counted the socks (six); Mrs. Tuomela's step-ins, folded modestly in half (two); two sets of one-piece men's union suits; a nightgown; a slip; and four men's handkerchiefs.

Then she sat at the counter at the front of the store and unrolled the envelope, rolled it in the opposite direction to flatten it, glanced out the front window but saw no cars, no customers, no passersby. She swallowed, slid a finger under the flap, pulled out a note card with a printed garland of pink daisies in the shape of a peace sign on the front. Noticing that the little circles that had danced above Cat's *i*'s and *j*'s in her letter of two years ago were missing, she began to read:

Dear Dale Ann,

This is very important. A friend of ours needs your help— it is something I can't put in writing. Would you please call me collect—the number is (312) 576-9938. Tell the operator that the call is from Linda, and we will know it is you. Call anytime. Please don't let anyone see this.

C

With the easy listening station on the radio playing over any creaks the wooden floor might make as she walked, Dale Ann stepped out of her shoes to tiptoe in stocking feet to the bedroom. The door had been left open a few inches, as it always was when Mr. Tuomela napped: she could see the old man lying fast asleep on his side of the bed, covered by a crocheted afghan that Grace had traded to Mrs. Tuomela for gas when she was out of cash. Mr. Tuomela didn't snore when he napped, so Dale Ann listened for his breathing— soft and light as a child's—and watched the orange and brown crocheted zigzags on his chest slowly rise and fall for a minute, then pulled the door until it was not quite closed, and walked silently back to the front of the store and the counter. She lifted the phone from its place next to the cash register and, gently stretching the cord as far as it would reach, took it into the small bathroom at the front of the store where she closed the door, sat on the floor, and dialed 0.

"Oppiter."

"I'd like to make a collect call."

"Number, please?"

"Three one two, five seven six, nine-nine-three eight."

"Who shall I say is calling?"

"Linda."

"One moment, please."

Keys tapped; faint beeps and chirps sounded on the line. Dale Ann held the receiver to her ear with her left hand, her right hand gripping the pink envelope, and her right arm crossed over her stomach at the waist.

bekaa boweting

THE PHONE RANG EIGHT TIMES.

"They do not answer; would you like to try again later?" the operator asked in her stilted voice. She added, more kindly, "Rates are lower after seven o'clock."

And then the receiver was picked up.

"Hello?" The young woman who answered sounded out of breath.

"I have a collect call from Linda. Will you accept the charges?"

"Yes, Operator, I will." It was not the desperately happy, silly voice that Dale Ann remembered, but it was Cat.

"Thank you. Go ahead, please."

A pause, then Cat asked, "Is she off the line? Can you talk?"

"Yes."

"Are you by yourself?"

"Yes." Again, Dale Ann paused. After all that happened she could think of nothing to say.

"You must have my note."

"Yes." And Dale Ann was silent.

"Will you promise you won't tell anybody about this?"

". . . All right. I promise."

A deep sigh. "It's—remember our friend whose name starts with *P*?"

Paul. How Dale Ann wished she didn't.

"I know there was something going on between you when you left here, but so much has happened since then. His grades were bad anyway, and he had some kind of trouble with his parents, and he stopped going to class and then he was dropped from school."

"Mmm," Dale Ann mumbled.

"I know . . . and it gets worse."

Dale Ann was silent, thinking, What do you mean, he had to get a job?

"He was drafted."

"He's in the Army?" Did he go to Viet Nam; had he been killed?

"When he got his draft notice he called his dad, and his dad told him to be a man, and he told his dad he wasn't going to go in the Army, and then his dad said then you're on your own, buddy . . . He tried to get classified as a conscientious objector but they denied it."

"Did he go, then?"

"No, he didn't go, and he's been staying with us. We thought nobody knew, but last week he got a letter from the draft board that his father had forwarded here, and then yesterday his father called. We said we hadn't seen him since he left school—and his father says he'll go to prison, and we will too, if we know where he is, so he's living somewhere else now. He says we can't know where but he'll call me . . . Are you still there?"

"Yes, I'm here."

"He's decided that he's going to Canada . . . Are you still there?"

"Yes." What do you want from me?

"How far are you from Canada?"

What do you want? Dale Ann didn't say the words.

"Can you help him get there? We have some money."

Silence.

"Are you still there? Don't hang up. Please."

After Eugene and Mrs. Tuomela returned from mail delivery, Dale Ann carried the five-pound brown paper sack of wild rice from Beryl Duhlebon into the store. "Do you want me weigh the rice and bag it?"

"I'll do it. See you in the morning, sweetheart. You get outside and enjoy this nice weather—while it lasts! You gonna play cards with Grace and Cecile and Cecile's boyfriend tonight?"

"If they need a fourth; Cecile's boyfriend might bring his little brother; otherwise, cribbage with my dad."

"Leave the inside door open a little, will you? Get some fresh air in here while the weather's nice."

Dale Ann left the heavier inside door open several inches and closed the screen door quietly behind her. Eugene, wiping dust from the chrome grill on the Buick, looked up when she said, "Cousin . . ."

Mrs. Tuomela weighed and rebagged the rice into half-pound plastic bags while Mr. Tuomela, fresh from his nap, turned the radio to Chmielewski Funtime on the polka station.

"I got a Polish boyfriend," Mrs. Tuomela sang along with Patty Chmielewski, "he looks a lot like you!"

"You do? Helmi! You never told me that before!" Mr. Tuomela did his best to sound shocked.

"I thought you'd just be jealous," his wife answered.

"He looks like me?"

"You could be twins!"

The old couple laughed, then Helmi said, "Will you look at that—Dale Ann is still here; she's out by the garage talking to Eugene!"

"What are they saying that looks so serious?"

"Don't wiggle the curtain, Jorma! We don't want them to know we're looking. Could be they're a little sweet on each other."

"Now, wouldn't that be something!"

Up until the accident, the plan had unfolded as if it was meant to be—and perhaps the accident itself was part of what was meant to be. The plan was that Paul would take the Greyhound from Chicago to Mesabi where he would be met by Dale Ann and Eugene, his hair no longer blond but dyed black. Before leaving Mesabi, Paul would hand Dale Ann a hundred dollars for the temporary use of an ID card, provided by Eugene, that he would use at the border crossing as proof that he was a Mozhay Pointer.

The three would then take the road to Sweetgrass as far as Miskwaa Rapids and Half-Dime Hill, then the lumber road to the Tweten cutoff that would bring them back to the highway just south of International Falls. At the crossing into Fort Frances, the three young Indians going into town for the day would show their IDs to border patrol, who would ask where they were born, what they were going to do in Canada, and how long they expected to stay. Once over the border they would travel on to Fort Frances, and before leaving Paul there downtown, Dale Ann would collect the ID card and another hundred dollars. The border patrol, if the same person was working, wouldn't remember how many Indians had been in the car earlier; Dale Ann and

Eugene would be just another young Indian couple on their way back to the reservation from a day trip to Fort Frances, with nothing to declare.

In downtown Mesabi, the young couple standing on the sidewalk outside the Finnish Cafe took care to stay out of the way and not block the doorway as they watched customers going into or leaving the restaurant. Although the day was warm the girl zipped her sweatshirt, pulled up the hood, and crossed her arms across her waist.

"Are you chilly?" the boy asked.

"Not really."

The boy took off his flannel-lined jean jacket and draped it over the girl's shoulders. "I'll get you some coffee, warm you up," he said and went into the cafe. From the sidewalk, Dale Ann watched him through the restaurant window that was steamy from conversation and cooking.

"What?" the cashier asked loudly. "Can't hear you! Coffee, did you say? It gets so noisy in here! Sugar and cream?"

"Yes, sugar and cream, thank you."

"To go, hon?"

Eugene nodded and stepped out of the way of the waitresses in white nylon work uniforms and pastel calico half-aprons hurrying from counter to booths to tables to take orders. Regulars requested their usual—coffee, bacon, eggs and toast, a bakery roll—and while talking about the weather, the son who got on at the mines, or last Friday's home football game, waited to watch passengers disembark from the Greyhound bus when it made its morning stop outside the cafe. Occasionally, an out-of-towner would exit the bus and walk into the cafe, where they would read the menu and, seeing no Finnish dishes listed, ask the waitress if there was a Finnish special.

"This is Mokros's restaurant," a waitress would explain. Mr. Mokros, the cook and owner, who would have been watching through the order, would smile, nod, and wave his spatula. The Greek, as he was known in Mesabi, had bought the Finnish Cafe decades earlier and had not changed the name; his theory was that it would be good for business in that part of the state.

"Oh," the confused customer would reply and order the eggs and toast.

Eugene waited patiently for the coffee, continuing to politely dodge the waitresses and other customers.

"What is that Indian girl doing staring into the window like that? Why doesn't she just take a picture?" This from the woman at the table in front of the window. She opened her menu and propped it onto the window still.

"She's with her boyfriend, I think. See him, the boy at the counter, the one with the Elvis hairdo?"

"Greaser. She probably can't trust him, thinks he'll try to pick up the waitress if she doesn't keep her eye on him." The first woman shifted, lifting her rear from the chair for a second or so to shift it so that her back would be to the window.

Inside, Eugene paid for the styrofoam cup of coffee and went back out to the sidewalk, where he handed the cup to Dale Ann. "The lady wrapped a napkin around it so you don't burn your fingers," he said.

"Here it comes," said Dale Ann, her voice tight.

All heads in the Finnish Cafe turned toward the front windows as the Greyhound bus pulled up in front and the driver opened the door.

Eugene and Dale Ann watched for a young man with

black hair as single file through the door passengers exited—
first a trio of teenage girls met by an older couple who might
have been their grandparents; a mother with several small
children; a half-dozen young men accompanied by two older
men in St. Louis County Jail jackets; a grandmotherly-looking
woman carrying a covered aluminum cake pan; and two sol-
diers in uniform, who went into the cafe for something to eat
while they waited for the bus to head farther north.

Paul's feet appeared first, heavy hiking boots with red
laces, then his legs, faded denim jeans with frayed hems.
Wearing a thick winter jacket too warm for fall, he carried
a bedroll that he set down on the sidewalk and adjusted his
aviator-style sunglasses as he looked to his left, to his right,
and into the windows of the Finnish Cafe. His wavy black
hair brushed his shoulders.

"Is that him?" Eugene asked.

"No." Dale Ann had forgotten for the moment that he had
colored his hair and was picturing instead the Paul of her last
evening in Chicago, the blond curls above the face that had
melted and imprinted invisibly and permanently into hers.
The Paul that she remembered had hazel-gray eyes and a
Cupid's-bow mouth with lips arched and pink; wet, smoky
breath, and an angry, tobacco-tasting tongue. And a scene
ignored by a careless God who had glanced at Dale Ann and
turned away, his mind on a falling sparrow perhaps.

"No," she said again, looking at the young man in the
winter jacket. The young man fidgeted with his sunglasses,
tucking the bows beneath the dark blue bandanna wrapped
across his forehead and tied in the back over his hair that
sprang up and bunched at the crown. He turned in Dale
Ann's direction, and the sunglasses fixed upon her. He
yanked the strap of an Army surplus duffel bag from the

luggage compartment under the bus, hoisted it onto his shoulder, and lifted one hand in a peace sign. Above the sunglasses his eyebrows raised and lowered uncertainly but unmistakably. It was Paul, of course.

"Yes, that's him." Dale Ann pushed her sweatshirt hood back. "Hi."

"Hey, Operator . . . are you still an operator?"

"No." Dale Ann cleared her throat awkwardly. "This is my cousin."

"Hey, man."

Eugene stuck out his hand, which necessitated Paul's setting down the duffel bag to shake it. "I'll get that," Eugene said politely, picking up the bag.

A man in a fatigue jacket walked too closely past Dale Ann, slightly brushing her shoulder and dropping a set of car keys on the sidewalk. "Excuse me, sorry," he apologized, bending to pick up the keys.

"Is that everything, then?" asked Eugene.

"Hey, I have to stop at the men's room first," said Paul. "Long bus trip."

"There's time; go ahead," Eugene answered.

Through the restaurant window Dale Ann saw Paul walk to the men's room at the back of the booths. The man who had dropped his keys exited the men's room door a minute later and sat at the counter, where he picked up a menu. A few minutes later, Paul opened the door and looked toward the man at the counter and the cashier, then walked past the rows of booths and tables, pausing at the counter, where he bought a pack of gum. The man in the fatigue jacket watched Paul leave the restaurant; through the window his and Dale Ann's eyes locked for split second before she looked away.

Eugene, Dale Ann, and Paul walked to the end of the

block and turned the corner, three friends disappearing from the sight of anyone who might remember them, toward the gravel parking lot behind the bar at the end of the next street where the Buick was parked. Eugene held the passenger door open for Dale Ann, and set the duffel bag onto the passenger side of the back seat, motioning with his head for Paul to enter on the other side. Except for gravel from peoples' shoes on the floor, the car was clean inside, the dashboard washed, and the windows, ashtrays, and door and window handles free of any prints or smears. A small green pine tree air freshener dangled from the cigarette lighter.

Old people car, thought Paul. "Kind of strong in here," he commented and rolled down the window.

"Close it," Eugene said in his low, husky voice.

Paul complied.

"You need to give Dale Ann three hundred dollars before we start. She'll give you the ID you can use, and when we get to Canada you give the ID back to Dale and she gives you a hundred dollars back."

"She can keep the ID until we get to the border, and I'll give her the two hundred dollars after we're in Canada."

Eugene's words were calm, unhurried: "Then you can get out."

Paul unhooked the strap from the duffel bag and felt the inside with one hand, pulling out a leather shaving kit that he partially unzipped. "No hassle, man," he said. "Operator wants her bread." He peered closely inside, his face partway into the kit, and opened a wallet, counting out bills that he crumpled in his fist. "Here, Operator." He thrust the bills toward Dale Ann. "You can count it if you want."

"Count it," said Eugene softly.

Dale Ann counted. The bills were damp and smelled of

shaving cream. "It's all here." She buttoned the money into her shirt pocket. "Here's the ID: you can have it now."

"I guess we're ready, then." Eugene started the car and turned on the radio. "Another thing, you'll need to sit low so it will look like there are only two people in the car."

Paul reclined onto his bedroll. "All right, Chief," he said, under his breath.

Eugene turned to look at the passenger in the back seat, who smiled sickly.

"Just a joke," he said lamely.

The Buick purred to a start and accelerated smoothly, turning from the alley to a side street, then several more blocks to County Road 5.

"We're going to take the road through the reservation, and then an old lumber road that will bring us back to the highway when we get about ten miles from International Falls," said Eugene. "The reservation road ends at the Miskwaa River; we'll stop to eat there, and after that I don't think we'll see anybody. You have to stay down until we get to the river. When we drive across the reservation, there's people who will recognize the car."

"We brought food: bologna and cheese, a loaf of bread, and a jug of Kool-Aid," said Dale Ann. "It's in the trunk."

"Far out," answered Paul, then, "I have candy bars and peanuts. And jerky. Would you like something?"

"I could eat a candy bar," answered Eugene, "if you'll unwrap it for me, Dale Ann."

Paul sat up from the duffel bag and dug inside. "Here's a Twizzler," he said as he handed a bar of red licorice to Dale Ann, then lay back down to recline on the bedroll. As she tore the top open and peeled the cellophane halfway down the bar, her stomach rolled and writhed at the scent of congealed strawberry and its pliant, bending warmth from

Paul's body lying on the duffel bag. She swallowed, handed the half-peeled bar to Eugene, and closed her eyes.

"Sun in your eyes? Pull down the visor," Eugene advised. "Paul, take out that driver's license; you'll need to know what's on it."

The driver's license was a white plastic card with raised blue lettering and a pattern of blue pine trees. Paul read the front, turned it over to read the back, then read from the front. "Michael Joseph Washington," he said from the back seat. "Minnesota license. He's a year older than I am."

"He's you now, or you're him, when we get to the border. They'll ask to see our IDs, and they might ask us our full names, birthdays, where we were born, where we live, and where we work, why we're going into Canada—you need to be ready."

"Where do I live?"

"You're from Mozhay Point and you live in Minneapolis, with your mother, Lucy Washington. You've been working at the Sonfish Bible Camp for the summer—that's on Sunfish Lake, just outside Mesabi where you got off the bus—and will be going back to Minneapolis after closing it down for the season. You're the handyman."

"I work at a Bible camp? Far out!"

"Your father's name is Joe Washington, and he lives at Mozhay Point," added Dale Ann.

"Dark brown hair, that's me . . . five-ten, a hundred seventy pounds . . . brown eyes, that's not me; mine are hazel."

"Keep your sunglasses on. If they ask you to take them off, you'll have to. I think you're close enough."

The Buick jumped over an uneven patch of road, changing gears. At the back of Dale Ann's eyelids, she was in a battered blue truck, seated between Zho Wash, who drove, and Beryl Duhlebon, staring dully past the road to Sweetgrass to the green-tiled walls of a hospital. Below the chatter of the weather forecast on the radio she heard a baby cry, hiccupping, unable to hold her head up from the harshly starched cotton of a nurse's shoulder. Exiting the hospital room the nurse turned a corner into the hallway and disappeared with Dale Ann's baby she imagined as a girl with ringlets as tight as Grace's, blonde curls that reflected the hospital's fluorescent lights to yellow gold.

The car approached the Dionne Fork, where Grace was shaking dust from a scatter rug into the yard, and across the road a middle-aged woman was sitting on the steps of the store with Mrs. Tuomela reading from a piece of paper. Eugene tapped the horn twice lightly and raised a hand to Grace at the left side of the car; Dale Ann did the same on the right to the women on the steps.

"Mrs. Minogeezhik—looks like she got a letter from Jack. Is he going to reenlist, do you know?" Eugene asked. "Last he wrote to me he said he might be stationed in Germany."

"Is that the HTH you had when you lived in Evanston? Is that his mother?" Paul raised his head.

"Keep down," instructed Eugene. "What's HTH?"

"Hometown honey—wasn't that his name, Jack?"

Eugene waited for Dale Ann to reply, interested in hearing her answer.

"We were just friends." Dale Ann's voice didn't quite crack, and she swallowed.

The car passed the Reservation Business Committee offices, a small log-sided building. In the parking lot, Waagosh McDougall, the committee secretary, leaned on the hood of his car, his hands cupped around a match as he lit a cigarette. Eugene tapped the horn again twice, and Waagosh nodded.

"It's not far now," said Eugene. "A few miles to Sweet-grass, and after that a few more miles to the river; the logging road is right there."

The radio announcer read the Pamida specials and played a slow song. "That was Patti Page, singing 'The Tennessee Waltz,' a request from Dorothy Nelson. Call in your favorite song to WMIR, or if you're in beautiful downtown Mesabi, stop by in person!"

"So, you're cousins?" This from Paul in the back seat. "You look alike."

"Our fathers are first cousins."

"So, you're what—second or third cousins? You look like brother and sister. Twins."

"You think so?" Eugene yawned to show his disinterest.

"It doesn't look like anybody's home at Sweetgrass," Dale Ann commented. Or was there? "Slow down, let me see; the sumac is so thick the driveway is almost covered." She wondered if Eugene had heard the rumor about Michael Washington and his ricing partner, that Margie Robineau from Duluth. "My mother heard that Margie Robineau, the girl who was ricing with Michael, is still there; Michael went to Minneapolis and she didn't go with. Then he went back to Mesabi for his job at that Bible camp, and she's still at Sweetgrass."

Dale Ann had heard that from her sister Yvonne. "Is she staying by herself? His dad's truck isn't there."

"The dogs will take care of anybody who bothers her." Eugene snorted. "There they are—the attack dogs! Unroll your window, will you, Dale Ann?" He called to the dogs, "Hey, Animooshag!"

Paul raised his head enough to see three or four dogs curled up at the base of a mailbox on a wooden sawhorse. Two of them, one a lab mix and the other a poodle mix, woke at the sound of Eugene's voice, squinted at the Buick, and closed their eyes; the others, large mongrels of no recognizable breed, stood and wagged their tails at the visitors.

"Look at those little ones; they're just tired out, exhausted, poor things," laughed Dale Ann. "Hard work, being Zho Wash's guard dogs." She peered down the driveway through the gaps in the sumac, looking for a girl watching Eugene's car through the front window of the house.

"You'll be able to sit up in a few minutes if you want," said Eugene toward the back seat. "We're coming to the boat landing on Lost Lake; there's probably nobody there since ricing is done. But just in case, I'll let you know when we're past the landing; after that there's no more blacktop, just dirt road. There's no houses after that, nobody else living out here who could see you."

Lying on his back Paul stretched his arms and rolled his head; his neck crackled. "What's ricing?"

"Wild rice, manoomin—you know what that is? It's ripe at the end of summer, and people go out on the lake to knock it off the stalks and into their boats. We sell some and eat the rest all year."

"I know what wild rice is; I've never seen where it came from."

"Well, go ahead and get up for a second and take a look. That's the boat landing; during ricing there's cars parked all along the road, and people camping out, hauling their boats down to the lake. You see everybody there. Once ricing's done, though, there's not much going on."

"It looks like a good place to stop and eat," said Paul.

"Naw, you never know who might decide to drive out here. It's not much farther to the rapids."

In the back seat, Paul dug into the duffel bag. "I've got the munchies," he explained. "Remember getting the munchies, Dale Ann?" He knelt on the back floor, his head between Dale Ann's and Eugene's as he watched the road. "Like the white rabbit said, feed your head," he said, exhaling the peanut-scented sweetness of a salted nut roll. Dale Ann rolled down her car window, turning her head from the warm wetness of his breath.

"You'll want to sit back on the seat; from here to the rapids, the road has some good-sized ruts." Eugene slowed the car as the road narrowed and curved sharply; the blacktop ended as they approached what appeared to be a wall of leaves.

"Man, it looks like everything is caving in."

Eugene steered carefully around first one rut, then another. "Where were you born?"

"Westchester."

"No, you're Michael Washington. Where were you born?"

"Mozhay Point. I work at the Bible camp. I love Jesus. How much farther?"

"We're close," said Dale Ann. "It's pretty—isn't it?—the leaves starting to turn yellow. When they fall this will be just bare branches, then once it starts to snow you can't get through here at all. They only plow as far as the boat landing."

"So, why is there a road here at all?"

"There used to be a fur trading post at the river, more than a hundred years ago, and a settlement where people lived. The road we're on now is how they got to Lost Lake to rice. And then to Odanang, the old settlement; nobody lives there now. Look straight ahead, you can see a little of the river now—see it?"

"What's your mother's name?" asked Eugene.

"Uh . . . Lucy. I live with her in Minneapolis."

The car negotiated one more turn, and suddenly the view on the driver's side cleared from brush and leaves to blue sky and a drop-off above an inlet framed by a flat U-shaped rocky beach. Below the inlet, a short stretch of slow rapids reflected the sky to a deeper, wavering blue that gave way to the rush of the Miskwaa River. On the opposite bank of the river, stands of trees thicker than the larches and popples that had lined the road from Sweetgrass appeared endless. On the passenger side, a steep hill blocked the sky, and the car stopped alongside the hint of an overgrown roadway—a crooked route branching off of the road from Sweetgrass between a dozen or so ancient-looking tamaracks, some dead or near death. In front of the car, the road from Sweetgrass widened somewhat and continued northward into the woods.

The three got out of the car, Dale Ann rolling her shoulders back and pressing her fists into the small of her back, Eugene patting his shirt pocket, and Paul stretching his arms above his head. "How long will it be until we get to Canada?" he asked.

"An hour and a half, not much more. That's the logging road, straight ahead. We'll take that to the Tweten cutoff, then come back out on the highway just south of International Falls."

"Are we stopping here to eat lunch?" Paul asked.

"I'm going down the shore, to the ridge," said Eugene. He patted his shirt pocket again. "You all right here?" He directed the question to Dale Ann, who nodded. "Back shortly, then," he said and walked into the brush, in the direction from which they had driven.

"It's wild out here," commented Paul. "Is he looking for a place to go to the bathroom?" He wondered, not so idly, if Eugene had been patting his shirt pocket to check for toilet paper.

Dale Ann walked to the drop-off and looked down at the inlet. "A long time ago when the fur post was here, down there is where the traders came with their pelts to trade. Back in the woods there, where you can see an old road, is where there was a little town called Odanang, with the trading post and houses all around it. It's gone now, just some old caved-in buildings back there. Well, there was a couple, a man and wife who were walking to Odanang and on the way they disappeared. Nobody ever knew what happened to them, but it was something bad. Eugene's great-grandfather, his mother's grandfather, is who found some of their clothes. His family visits there sometimes and they put down tobacco. It's a prayer, a remembrance."

"Spooky." Paul tossed a small rock off the drop-off into the inlet, then picked up a larger rock and heaved it into the water, where it made a cracking sound as it hit other rocks.

"Don't do that," said Dale Ann. "We don't do that here."

"More spooky stuff?" Paul stood next to Dale Ann and looked down at the top of her head. "You haven't grown any taller, have you, Operator?" He recalled that he had had to stoop slightly to run his hands along her sides, pulling up her flannel nightgown, the kind that the grandmother wore in the Little Red Riding Hood book he'd had as a child; underneath she had worn large, drooping cotton underpants. Urgency had tempered revulsion, revulsion tempered urgency, and urgency had prevailed.

Dale Ann said nothing.

"Do you ever hear from your roommates, besides Cat writing to you last month?" Paul took a step closer, his arm inches from hers.

"No." Buff had written to request that Dale Ann send her a check for thirty dollars for her share of the telephone bill. She had folded the check into a page from an advertising circular and mailed it.

"Cat is cool, but that Buff was bogus. What a phony rich-bitch, lording it over everybody. Remember how she always left her debutante album sitting out so people would pick it up and ask, What's this? Some made-up country club her dad joined because they couldn't get into a real one. Cat wouldn't let anybody make fun of her." Paul picked up another rock and set it down. "Oh, right, don't throw rocks," he said and stroked Dale Ann's hair away from her face.

"I don't remember much."

"That's cool. I don't either." Paul continued to stroke her hair. "I have a joint in my pocket, the last one before I cross into Canada; can't risk trying to bring anything across. Would you like to share it? Your cousin doesn't have to know."

"Did you know that I had a baby?"

Paul drew back his hands, palms toward Dale Ann.

"Did you know that?"

He sighed. "How do you think I ended up here? Of course I knew it. You're the one who gave my name to a social worker, and the county government got ahold of my dad. He ended up paying out a lot of money—did *you* know *that*?—for the hospital, and then for somebody to adopt it so he wouldn't have to keep paying for it. And I got kicked out of school for my grades, and he wouldn't give me anything to go to State, told me to go to work and pay for it myself. And then I got drafted, and he wouldn't help me there either, told me it was time I started acting like a man—like him, he meant. If it wasn't for Cat, I would be on my way to Viet Nam."

"So you know what happened to the baby, where it is?" Dread and hope sank like mercury to the pit of her stomach. She felt her bladder fill and wondered if she would be able to keep from wetting her pants.

"Why would I want to know that? Why would you even

bring it up—aren't things bad enough? All this shit started with you—you wanted it, and then you didn't, and you gave my name to a social worker, and you ruined my life, Dale Ann. You ruined it." Paul was weeping. "You did. Ruined my fucking life."

"Where is the baby, Paul?"

"Didn't you hear what I said? Somebody adopted it. Nobody knows." Paul's face, close to hers, had reddened; his mouth worked as he held back his sobs. Lips quivering, he said, "Don't you get it? Everything is fucked up because of you," which Dale Ann had known all along.

The Miskwaa River stopped flowing and the rapids stilled as Dale Ann recognized that Paul's words were true.

Paul picked up a rock and put his weight on his right foot. Twisting his body with his right arm back, he shifted to his left foot while he threw—across the river was his intention, to the other side, to the freedom he had lost because of a girl he disliked.

Wordlessly, Dale Ann watched the rock leave his hand and arc over the inlet—where it stopped, suspended in mid-air as Paul stopped, suspended at the edge of the dropoff, as still and frozen in the moment as the rock. Dale Ann heard the earth at the side of Half-Dime Hill shift and sand scatter down toward the abandoned settlement, where trees shuddered and shed their leaves, leaves that stopped before they reached the ground. At the drop-off where she and Paul stood the air began to vibrate, then shake; the rock Paul had thrown fell from its arc and hit the surface of the inlet without a sound, and the edge of the drop-off began to crumble. Below, the river resumed its flow, accelerating to a rush: Bekaa Boweting, the slow-moving rapids roiled; all in silence, it seemed.

Paul pivoted, shuffled his feet. "Dale Ann," he begged, "give me your hand."

She unfolded her arms that were crossed over her middle, where the baby had grown and once born had left empty, reluctantly extending a hand that was pale, cold, and that grew in size as it neared Paul, the nails ragged, their bases crusted red-brown. Fascinated, she watched the skin on that hand and arm form wrinkles, purple veins rising, seeking; she felt that she was thirsty. Paul's face, incredulous and upturned, now several feet below hers. He opened his mouth; the wet, rosy flesh of his tongue and gums surely led to more of the same inside; she felt that she was hungry. Her hand inching toward his, Dale Ann stretched, flexed her fingers and rolled her shoulders, and looked with her own dead eyes into Paul's living and frightened ones, playing for him the scene she had played in her mind over and over until he had stopped and pulled her damp and creased flannel nightgown back down over her thighs: a girl on a single cot staring dry-eyed at a square white light fixture that became a lace handkerchief on snow, a snare stepped on by a deer who hung, front hooves dangling, bleeding onto the snow.

"Waabindan," she said silently.

Behind the black frames of her Indian Health Service glasses, lightning reanimated Dale Ann's eyes, shedding blue sparks that fell like tears. Behind the thickness of heavy glass lenses, violet clouds glowed and reddened, then faded. She withdrew the hand and placed it at the top of her abdomen, where both hands had rested, fingers intertwined, above the tiny being she had carried.

"Weweni," she whispered, her face curiously Madonna-like.

the etienne store

EUGENE HAD FOLLOWED THE PATHWAY near the riverbank to the ridge outside the abandoned settlement at the foot of Half-Dime Hill. The pathway was an erratic route that dipped into mud in some places and rose to masses of dead tree roots in others, never an easy trek. In the time of the removals of the Muskrats and other nontreaty families from Sweetgrass to the unallotted lands along the river, that had been the route those families had taken to trade at the Etienne store at the settlement. There were rumors that the pathway, like the settlement, was haunted; as far as anyone knew, the only people to set foot on it in decades were the Dionne men: Eugene had walked it since he was a small boy with his father and grandfather.

He had heard the story many times and would be able to retell it to his own children and grandchildren, with the proper sequence, detail, and cadence used by his own father and grandfather. Recounting to himself he noted the seasonal changes since the last time he had been on the path in early summer—his father had put tobacco down at the bases of several aging tamaracks, commenting only that they had been there a long time. Eugene had understood that they were being honored for their age and all that they had seen and heard during their lifetimes.

His father had then picked up a small, round stone and

held it in his hand for a moment, then set it back down in its place, and Eugene understood that the stone was also being honored and respected.

"Just think how long this rock has been here," his father had said, "right here, near that ridge," and began to speak of that day years ago when his own grandfather, sixteen-year-old Antoine Dionne, sent by his older brothers to check their illegal traplines, had seen what he had first thought was a large crow atop a snowbank, its feet frozen into the snow, wings flapping and body swaying in distress. It appeared to be straining toward the lowest branches of a large white pine that seemed to wave and sway in sympathy with the frenzied bird.

Wondering if he could help free the crow, Antoine had stepped cautiously closer and saw that it was not a bird at all but a green plaid shawl like the one worn by Liza Washington frozen halfway into the snowbank. With his hands the boy pulled the shawl free and dug the crusted snow away from a half-buried willow basket beneath it. Underneath that was a man's red velvet cap and a skin bag filled with uneaten dried venison. He recognized the hat, made by Joseph Washington's mother, who fashioned the tam full and deep enough to cover Joseph's ears on cold days.

"Joseph Washington!" Antoine called. "Joe Muskrat!" There was no answer, no sound but for the wind winding and snapping through branches of white pine. He spread the shawl on top of the snow and placed the basket and skin bag inside, then brushed and shook ice and snow from the folds of the hat. Red dye melted and ran from the fabric, marking his fingers.

"Joe Washington! Little Muskrat!" Wiping his nose on the back of his hand he smelled a familiar stale rustiness that brought to his mind the carcass of a deer that had been attacked by wolves; horrified at the scent of blood he dropped the hat and ran, forgetting the bundled shawl.

The next day Antoine returned to the ridge with his older brothers to search for Joseph and Liza. The oldest brother, Maxime, carried a gun, barrel down and ready to cock; the largest, Mizhaa, a kettle of lard; and the youngest brothers, Antoine and Michel, an armload each of firewood and kindling that they lit as soon as they arrived, setting the kettle on top to melt the lard. If a Windigo had attacked the couple, it might still be in the vicinity and hungry for more human flesh. If that should happen, the men would have to try to kill it by pouring boiling lard down its throat, the only way known.

The snow on the ridge was covered with a thin crust of ice but nothing else. Next to it the white pine shaded the ridge that was empty except for the snow. Like Joseph and Liza, the shawl, cap, willow basket, and skin bag had disappeared. The men built a fire, heated the lard, and cautiously looked for any signs of husband and wife or evidence of their demise, calling their names, at first softly. Then, as the air kept its slow wintry sweep, the ground didn't shake, and the surface of the melted lard remained smooth, the calls grew to shouts: "Joseph! Joe Muskrat! Liza!"

Before the sun began to set, the fire died under the kettle and the lard congealed to a whiteness that matched the sky. The men left the ridge and returned home.

For the rest of his life—and he lived to be an old man— Antoine wondered if, had he not run so quickly, he might have retrieved the shawl, cap, kettle, and skin bag for their son, young Zho Wash. In the first several years afterward Antoine felt fearful at times of the outdoors, of what menace might be behind the movements of shadows or the patterns of sunlight through leaves. He could not wash the scent of blood from his hands, although he rubbed them with moss and crushed pine needles between his palms countless times—when he brought his fingers close to his nose he smelled the rotten rustiness that clung to his skin. In time, he began to inhale deeply of those things that would touch his body or that he would eat or drink: his shirt and his moccasins when he dressed in the morning, the wooden axe handle before and after he chopped wood, and his food, the last pretending that he was sniffing in appreciation.

Therese LaForce, Half-Dime's ancient mother and the oldest elder in the extended family communities of both Miskwaa Rapids and Mozhay Point, noticed Antoine's peculiar habit, giving a quick look as he closed his eyes and pressed his nose into a piece of lugalette.

"Ahhh, nothing like Artense's fresh lug," he said, opening his red-rimmed, exhausted eyes.

Knowing that there was indeed nothing quite as overworked, tough, and salty as her daughter-in-law's lugalette, she said quietly, "Ningosis, is there something troubling you?"

Antoine had never heard the old woman address anyone as grandson, and he nearly wept at the endearment and began to tell her all that had been troubling him. As she listened, Therese occasionally wiggled her child-sized moosehide moccasins—she was rather vain of her feet—and crossed and uncrossed her tiny-boned ankles, which were tied girlishly with colored tape at the bottoms of her black wool leggings. She drew on her dainty clay pipe from time to time, saying, "Mmmm hmmm . . . mmmm hmmmm" encouragingly.

When Antoine had finished the two sat quietly for some time, Therese giving thought and Antoine's spirit resting in relief, comfort, and hope. The clay pipe grew cold; she tapped the bowl into her left palm and scattered the ash into the air, then carefully tucked the clay pipe into the small leather bag she wore tied to her waist. The silver crucifix that she had been given by her grandmother before she died swung slightly from its spot over where her breasts had been when she was younger; the burnished surface and corpus captured the orange light of the sunset, flashed, and reflected it back to the sky. "I could be wrong, but this is what I am thinking . . ." she began.

For the rest of his life Antoine visited the ridge from time to time, putting down tobacco at the base of the white pine, between its roots that rose above the soil as years passed. Each time he recalled Therese's counsel, that the Great Spirit God the Creator made all beings—humans, animals, birds, fish, and insects—and all spirits, and that each was created with reason and for a purpose. We can ponder the creation of Windigo—why such a spirit?—but we must accept that it is something beyond our understanding as humans. Perhaps we might someday acquire this knowledge, and perhaps not. In the meantime, the Great Spirit God the Creator intended that we should do what we can to live good lives, to walk a good path in a good way.

When Therese had finished speaking, the two sat in a comfortable and holy silence for a short time. Antoine wondered how he could express his gratitude; he had nothing tangible to give.

"Migwech, Nokom," he said, addressing her as "Grandmother," the term of greatest honor for an elder and mindimooyenh.

Therese nodded graciously.

"Is there a word for more than migwech? A word for how much this means to my heart and my spirit?"

"Ningosis, Grandson, *Migwech* is always enough."

"I am thinking," said Antoine, "that what I will do is honor their memory, Joseph and Liza, by visiting that place. From the ridge a person can look across Bekaa Boweting to the other side of the river; a person can feel sheltered beneath the branches of the white pine that watches over their spirits; a person can put down tobacco by the roots of the white pine and pray."

This custom of visiting the white pine was passed to the generations of Dionne men who followed: Antoine to his son Mishaa, who passed it to his son George, who passed it to Eugene. Each man in the succession kept the tradition: from Antoine down to Eugene, no Dionne man had encountered a Windigo, or any traces of an encounter, but they understood that the visit and prayer were not for their own protection but a reaffirming of and commitment to the honor and courage that are the gift and obligation of Ojibwe men.

So it was that Eugene, before eating the lunch of bologna, bread, and Kool-Aid packed in the trunk of the Buick, had left Dale Ann with Paul to walk to the ridge that had been watched and prayed over by the Dionne men and the white pine.

He had tapped his shirt pocket to check for the pouch of Half and Half and walked the invisible pathway that he had learned from his father, bearing south to the flat-topped boulder Adoopowin, then eastward and crossed the shallow ravine, jumping across the muck at the bottom to keep his shoes clean, then turning south again to reach the white pine and the ridge. He looked across the slow rippling of Bekaa Boweting toward the dense greenery on the other side of the Miskwaa River, then placed a pinch of tobacco between the large roots of the white pine, where he prayed his acknowledgment of thanks for all the gifts from the Creator, for the Washington family, and that everyone, including Eugene himself, would live good lives.

"Migwech," he said in closing. "Gigawaabimin minawaa, zhingwaak," he said to the tree, touching the bark and then his heart, "I'll see you again."

On the walk back Eugene was observant, as his father had advised him to be when in the vicinity of the ridge, and at the same time thoughtful. Some of the trees had begun to shed leaves; a yellowing aspen leaf drifted down slowly, brushing his face in its descent to the earth, then another and still another fell to the path in front of his feet. Before long the nearly invisible path would be covered with leaves, and not long after that snow. When he visited the ridge in winter, Eugene's tracks would remain in the snow each time until a new snowfall. He wondered at the absence of tracks when Antoine and the uncles had returned to the ridge searching for Joseph and Liza Washington. It may have been that a Windigo had attacked the couple, or their disappearance was due to other circumstances that would never be known.

"And what about Joseph and Liza?" Eugene startled himself by speaking the words aloud, then continued his thoughts silently. *Why would the Creator, who made everything and knows all that will happen, allow such a terrible thing to happen? A husband and wife, who never caused any troubles to anyone and lived good lives, why would the Creator allow their children, Joe and Susan, such loss? Susan dying at such a young age, and Zho, at boarding school and then wounded in the war, a great spiritual leader—was this awful thing a part of the Creator's plan to lead him here?*

In his walk back to the car, Eugene thought that one day

he might ask the Creator these things directly in his prayers. He would ask Zho Wash first for guidance, if it wouldn't make the elder feel too sad to return to the tragedy.

His mind stilled, Eugene suddenly realized that the air around him had stilled as well. Leaves had stopped falling and tree branches had stopped swaying, in the absence of any wind at all. He began to sweat—was this not a sign of the approach of a Windigo, this dead stillness, followed by a vibration that caused trees to tremble, small animals to quiver and flee? He thought of Dale Ann: had she unwrapped the bologna, how far could the scent of food carry without any wind? How much time did they have to get into the car and drive away? He calmed himself by breathing slowly and evenly, and sped his steps smoothly and quietly, to be less noticeable to any predator, Windigo or other.

Winded after a stretch, Eugene stopped to catch his breath, and as he did so the leaves began to fall from the trees again, branches resumed their movement, and he felt air move across his face. And then he was at the small clearing where the Buick was parked at the side of the road, and Dale Ann was standing alone at the edge of the drop-off, looking down at the inlet and its narrow shoreline, where canoes paddled by voyageurs, traders, and Ojibwe men and women had stopped to load and unload pelts, kettles, cloth, needles and thread, and perhaps even Therese LaForce's grandmother's silver crucifix.

"Dale Ann," called Eugene.

She stood motionless, with her arms crossed at her waist, staring downward at the sharp black rocks that lined the shore below the ridge, where Paul was lying on his back with his arms above his head, his legs splayed out from the right hip, as if both had been joined there.

Eugene whistled sharply, and Dale Ann startled like a deer. Suddenly afraid that she could leap from the ridge, he sprinted down the invisible path toward the ridge, stopping at the spot that had been the entryway from the inlet to the settlement.

"Little cousin," he said quietly and linked his arms through hers until he felt her body relax, then together they climbed down and walked back along the inlet shore to where Paul lay.

His eyes were closed. Was he unconscious? Dale Ann placed a hand on Paul's chest, which didn't rise or fall; Eugene felt the boy's neck for a pulse, touched his face, and carefully turned his head to one side, then the other, where it stayed, a small trickle of blood running from his left nostril to his cheek and onto Eugene's hand.

"Little cousin . . . ," he began.

"Your hands," said Dale Ann. "Look at your fingers; his nose is bleeding." Her face was expressionless, her pupils dilated.

Eugene looked down at his hands, then calmly stood and walked to the water's edge, where he splashed and rubbed them together, then wiped them on the sides of his pants, looking across the river to the frieze of tamaracks on the other side. He might have thought to himself that he had always loved Dale Ann and always would, but that love was so deeply embedded into his very being that the thoughts and words would have been superfluous, and for the moment wasted time when there was no time to waste.

"We're going to move the car into the woods," he said. "Let's go; wewiib, probably nobody will come out here, but we have to make sure nobody can see us if they do."

Together, Eugene and Dale Ann walked to the car, and

Eugene drove it along the path until it was almost obscured from the road by sumac trees, thick and low, and just beginning to turn color. "If anybody sees the car they might think we're making out, the way I've got it nosed into the bushes like that, or if they come to look, they'll think that we're out in the woods. We'll hear them if they do. I'm going to put the duffel bag on the floor in the back seat and lock the doors, just in case, and we'll take the bedroll down to the water."

Together, Dale Ann and Eugene wrapped Paul's body in the bedroll blanket and half-lifted, half-dragged it to the abandoned settlement, to the shed behind the old Etienne house, at the base of Half-Dime Hill. Together, they pulled aside the brush that had grown over the door, and then Eugene shouldered the door open. Inside the dark windowless shed were a broken bucket, several pieces of lumber, a rusted saw, a heavy work table, and a wooden chair with three legs.

"I can get him in there myself; you go get the duffel bag and bring it here," Eugene directed.

When Dale Ann returned with the duffel bag, Paul was on the work table, lying as if he were asleep on half of the bedroll, the other half draped across his lower body. With the door open, in the semidarkness his face looked babyish; his mouth had fallen slightly open; he might have been asleep.

"Here's his sunglasses." Dale Ann slid them into Paul's shirt pocket and placed his folded boonie hat next to his head. "He left his hat in the car."

"We're going to have to go through the duffel bag." Eugene squeezed the carabiner clip and began to pull out the contents, which he placed on the ground outside the door: another pair of jeans, a sweatshirt, several pairs of socks, undershirts and briefs, a bath towel, a pair of tennis shoes tied together at the laces, two paperback books (*One Flew over the Cuckoo's Nest* and a novel with the title *Turn*

Me On!), a muffler, a tan raincoat, a turtleneck sweater, and a dopp kit. Inside the kit were a razor, toothbrush, a tube of Crest toothpaste, a crushed roll of toilet paper, an aerosol can of Right Guard deodorant, several loose dollar bills, a bar of soap, a washcloth, and a box of Vicks cough drops, already opened. A few triangular, brown, translucent pieces of something were scattered in the kit, along with others that were square, a lighter shade of brown in color, and had a grainy finish.

"Hash," said Dale Ann. "Hashish."

"Do you eat it?"

"No, you smoke it. It's like pot but stronger."

What kind of people had she been living with in Chicago, Eugene thought, and why would that relocation worker, that woman with the silly giggle that Dale Ann's mother treated like the Queen of England, place a girl like Dale Ann there?

"That stupid asshole—he was going to try to take it across the border?" asked Eugene. "Do you know what would have happened if they decided to search the car? We would have all gone to prison! Is there anything else in the bag?"

"There's a pocket inside." Dale Ann unzipped it. "It's papers . . . No, it's money—Eugene, it's money. It looks like a lot of money."

"How much?"

Dale Ann riffled the bills through her hands. "I can't tell."

"Can you take it outside to count it?"

"Come with me."

Dale Ann and Eugene knelt on the damp ground outside the shed and counted ones, fives, tens, and twenties. "It's six hundred and thirty dollars, Eugene."

"Put it in your pocket."

"No—you take it."

"All right, I'll hold it for now. Pack the other stuff back into the shaving kit, and we'll put that and everything else in the duffel bag."

They left the duffel bag in the corner of the shed and Paul on the table. Eugene pulled the door shut and pushed brush and pieces of broken boards in front of it. "Nobody has been here in more than fifty years, I bet, and nobody will come here for another fifty." He took his comb from his pocket and shaped his hair back into an Elvis quiff, sides combed in scallops toward the back, top pushed forward, a ducktail in the back.

"Let's go," he said.

They turned the car around and drove east toward home, the Dionne Fork. As they neared Lost Lake, Dale Ann asked if they could stop for a minute at the landing. She got out of the car and bent over, her hands on her knees. Gulping air, "I'm all right, I'm all right," she said to Eugene, waving away his arm that he was placing around her waist. "So thirsty . . . ," she said faintly, back in the Buick's passenger seat.

"We'll get you a 7 Up at the store," said Eugene. "Will it help to open your window?"

Dale Ann cranked her window down and stuck her head out to the side, closing her eyes as the wind blew her hair back. Eugene thought a joke might help. "Hey, my dog likes to ride like that."

She sat upright then and looking straight ahead asked, "Do you remember what a sin of omission is?"

"From catechism class? Yes, I do."

"I could have kept him from falling."

At the fork, Eugene parked in front of the gas station. "Come in with me and I'll buy you a 7 Up," he said. "Dale Ann, that money is for you. You can use it to go to school. It will get you started, and I'll help you."

part iii.
noongoom, 2022

Remains Discovery in Miskwaa River State Park

The St. Louis County Sheriff's Department has confirmed that the body of a deceased individual has been discovered in the Miskwaa River State Park. No further details are available at this time. The case is under investigation.

Duluth News Tribune (September 27, 2022)

Body Discovered in Miskwaa River State Park

An anonymous source in the Mozhay Point Tribal Government Center has verified that the body found in the Miskwaa River State Park is a long-deceased male. Items found with the body include identification information. A statement will be forthcoming from the Mozhay Point Division of Law Enforcement and the St. Louis County Sheriff's Department.

The Timberjay, serving Northern St. Louis County (October 26, 2022)

the laforce allotment

WHILE EVERYONE ELSE STAYED at the visitor center and off the trails, no one questioned or stopped Dale Ann Minogeezhik, the Mozhay Point tribal chairman's wife, as she accompanied her husband and Michael Washington into the old Odanang settlement. Michael led the way along the long-overgrown path to the Etienne house that had in other times also been the post office, store, and trading post. Hesitating, Dale Ann stopped as the men turned the corner of the house, calming herself by touching her hair, its color a near-black sable shot through with natural silver strands, newly styled the day before. The swirls and crests of the waves, peaking at the top and sides, had not moved. "Everything is under control," she said to herself, feeling oddly and coldly agitated in her apprehension. To slow her breathing and heartbeat she leaned against a solid-looking aspen, next to and unaware of Beryl Duhlebon, who at the curve of the path was unfolding the lawn chair of her elder, Therese LaForce, and Rose Sweet, who was holding Therese's tin coffee cup.

"The ground is good and level here, eyaa?" Beryl asked, wiggling the chair. "Namadabin, daga, Nokom."

"It's plenty good, Beryl," said Therese, her tiny behind taking up perhaps half of the webbed seat. She fluffed out the

skirt of her black wool dress to each side, smoothed the col-
ored tape ribbon trim on the bottom of the skirt, and wrapped
the open sleeves of her matching jacket over her chest. "Andii
Shigogoons?"

Artense, the name she preferred over her childhood nick-
name, appeared from around the corner of the Etienne house.
"Here, Mother; I was just looking around the store, and our
house, remembering all the nice things we had before we
moved to the allotment." She unfolded her lawn chair and sat
gingerly, checking its stability. "Well, we took what we could."

Dale Ann lightly traced the swirl of hair over her forehead,
then unwrapped a stick of gum that she began to chew.
Her jaw clicked; she spit out the gum and took several
steps along the path and paused, her arms wrapped across
her stomach and her attention on the shed. For less than
a second, Grace Dionne stepped invisibly onto the path,
directly in front of Dale Ann, then mother walked through
daughter and disappeared.

"Coming, Dale Ann?" asked Jack from the shed in back
of the Etienne house.

"Yes, I'm right behind you," she said.

"Kwewag, I have asked Grace to sit with us today," said Beryl.
"She is Dale Ann's mother, after all, and I thought she should
be here. She said that she would bake chocolate chip cookies to
go with the coffee."

"I wish somebody would have told us we would still be eat-
ing those tooth-breakers after we passed," said Rose. "I could
have prepared myself." Artense snickered.

A low tamarack branch at the side of the path nearly

brushed Grace's head as she strode up to the group. "Am I late? I was waiting for the cookies to cool." As she had in life, she wore a bleached white dish towel wrapped turban-style over her pin curls, and as she had so many times in life, she held a bowl of irregular brown lumps with a sheen of Crisco from the cookie sheet against her chest with one hand; the other hand gripped a mug with MOZHAY POINT BAND OF CHIPPEWA: WORLD'S BEST WILD RICE AND MAPLE SYRUP *written on the side.*

"Coffee, everyone? Grace, you went to all the trouble for us, migwech," said Artense, whose cheeks still carried a blush of pride from her mother's compliment about her throwing arm when she'd thrown the rock.

Grace leaned her unfolded lawn chair against the trunk of a tamarack.

"Aren't you going to sit, Grace?" asked Beryl solicitously.

"Gawiin." Grace tugged at the back of her turban, which felt tight.

"I just love cookies dunked in coffee, don't you?" asked Beryl.

"Much easier on the teeth," said Rose.

"Inabin gaye biizindan, daga." Therese, who could not spare another tooth, dropped her cookie into her cup, where it floated until saturated with makade mashkiki waboo, then sank to the bottom, where it would soak and soften.

"The ice bucket that the guy dropped is sitting on the roof of the shed back of the house," said Michael. "We can get to it easy; half of the roof has slid right. But there's some other stuff there, too, that Martin is going to have to see. I think you might want to ask him to close the park for the rest of the day."

At the top of Half-Dime Hill, directly above the Etienne house and shed, the stranded hikers were being directed by

Ranger Scott Martin and EMT Dag Bjornborg to stay exactly as they were, to not let go of the cedar tree, and especially not to move their feet. A rope had been secured around the trunk of a poplar at the top of the hill; the ranger and Dag gripped and loosened the rope as Tyler, the younger EMT, descended in climbing gear to the couple, Merrilee and Ann watching over the edge of the hill and talking steadily to the man and woman. "We're going to pull you up to the top of the hill; you'll be fine, just breathe easy and don't move. Tyler is bringing a harness; he will help you into it and will bring you up, one at a time," Merrilee called down to the couple. "The lady first, okay?"

"Can somebody look for the urn?" The man directed his shout toward the shed. "It's an antique, worth a lot of money! Is anybody down there?"

"Below you! We're below you!" Jack shouted up the hillside from the shed. "We see where it is; we're going to try to retrieve it!"

"Well, look for the lid, too, will you, and be careful with it!"

"For God's sake, Lyle, just hold on to the damn tree, will you!" hollered his wife, suspended twenty feet above his head, arms wrapped around Tyler. "By the way, I'm Bev," she said conversationally.

"Pleased to meet you, ma'am," said Tyler, his eyes on Merrilee and the rope.

"Bev," she said flirtatiously.

Lyle called down the hill. "Did it get scratched?"

"What the hell does he expect it's going to look like?" asked Jack. The urn had followed the ashes of the cremains, but where the ashes had flown and scattered, the urn had rolled and bounced, landing finally on what was left of the shed roof.

"Here it is, Chief." Jack pointed with his chin toward the shed. Part of the remainder of the roof had slid onto the ground and part into the shed. The contents visible through the hole in the roof—a table, a broken chair, and assorted boards and rusted tools—were covered with mildew and debris. "It's on the table."

"Jesus," said Jack. At one end of the table was a hat, at the other end a laced boot, both moldy. Between, the length of the table was covered by a debris-scattered blanket over a form that looked human. "What the hell?"

"Yeah," said Michael. "What do you think?"

Dale Ann stood still and unblinking as she stared into the shed. She remembered Eugene saying, "Nobody has been here for at least fifty years; it will probably be another fifty years before anybody else is." At twenty, fifty years was such a distance into the future—endless, she would have thought at the time.

"Tell you what," said Jack as he placed an arm around his wife's shoulders. "I'm going to talk to Scott after they get those people off the hill. He's going to want to close the park for the day and call the sheriff . . . You all right, Dale Ann? Awful thing to see; let's get out of here. Michael, you can stay here, keep people away till the park gets closed, all right?"

"Yeah. In the meantime I'll get the goddamn trophy cup off the roof and look around to see if I can find a lid," said Michael.

Bev and Lyle having been successfully hoisted to the top of Half-Dime Hill, the ranger directed Merrilee and Ann to go back to the visitor center and call Mozhay Point Facilities to send an ATV to help bring the couple back down. While the women took the long way down the less steep, stable northern side of the hill, Dag checked Bev and Lyle to see if they were all right physically. Scott spoke sternly to the now-hatless couple about straying from the trails, past the signs, and about dumping someone's cremated ashes on what had been people's homes.

"Lyle's brother felt so deeply about the Native Americans; he really identified with their spirituality, and he wanted his ashes to be scattered over an ancient Indian burial ground," Bev explained. "We were going to the park anyway, and since no one has lived in the Indian village for a long time, really, would it really matter that much to the park or to the old village? It's not as though everybody else is doing it." She winked as she smiled confidingly at the ranger.

Scott's face was expressionless. "I'm going to cite you right here. You'll be hearing from the Park Service and the Mozhay Point Tribal Council about possible charges," he answered, "and probably a fine and reimbursement for the expense of the EMTs and the rescue vehicles. I'll need to see your park pass. You have a park pass, right?"

"Of course we do," said Bev, no longer smiling.

An hour later Jack returned to the Etienne house with Deputy Sheriff Sonny Strand, but without Dale Ann. Waiting by the shed were Margie, Scott, and Dag, who would be transporting the body in the medic van to the coroner's office in Duluth, and whose discretion could be trusted. The deputy took statements from Jack and Michael and photographed the body, the shed, and objects, including a duffel bag found nearby, half-buried in mud and wet leaves.

"We will need to smudge and to say a prayer for his journey, and for his life on the other side," said Margie, taking a small pouch from her pocket.

"Can't put anything on the body or anywhere near it; this may be a crime scene," said the sheriff.

"Just a prayer, then," said Margie, who held the pouch in one hand. She circled the table, bending closely four times as she prayed from each direction.

Donning gloves, the men slid the body onto an open bag laid out on a gurney, then zipped the bag closed. As the men loaded the gurney into the back of the rescue van, Dag thought to himself, *Some hiker, some kid out by himself looking the place over, probably thought he would sleep in the shed. What could have happened to him? That wavy hair like Joey's—he probably wasn't much older than Joey is now.* Who was the young man's family, and who had missed him? Unexpectedly, the young man's death seemed personal to Dag, a grief falling like rain from a cloud that had waited too long to release. Dag thought he might weep. *We'll take the best care of him we can,* Dag promised the young man's people as he began the drive to Duluth.

"What next, Sonny?" asked Michael.

"I'll take the duffel bag for now," said the deputy, unfolding another body bag. "You'll need to help—keep your gloves on before you touch anything." He opened the bag and spread it on the ground next to the table where the body had been, then secured the carabiner at its base to the grommets at the top of the bag with several zip ties. "We'll lift on three," he directed. "I'll take one end and you can both take the other to the squad; we're going to put it in the back seat. Keep your gloves on until we're all through."

Zipped, the plastic bag looked as though there were a body inside. Michael felt a little queasy; Scott made a sign of the cross. With the screen and window between the front and back seats, Sonny drove as carefully as though the body were a living person.

*

The next day Jack received a call from Sonny Sweet: in preparation for the autopsy, an identification card had been found on the body, a long-expired Minnesota driver's license issued to Michael Joseph Washington of Mesabi, Minnesota.

"It gives a birthdate of August 9, 1949, height five feet ten inches, weight 170 pounds, dark brown hair and eyes, no corrective lenses required."

In a split second, Jack's thoughts were on the election, the recreation center, and the LaForce family allotment lands. "Mmmm," he answered, his voice noncommittal and his face as expressionless as if the conversation were in person.

"There's not another Michael Washington, is there?" the sheriff asked.

"Not that I know. Did they find anything else?" Had Michael screwed something up?

"Some money, a few bills, and some change. It probably had been in his shirt pocket—hard to tell, the coroner says. Look, we're going to need to talk to Michael. ASAP."

"I'll tell him; we'll come right there."

During the drive to the sheriff's office, Michael swore that he knew nothing about the dead hiker. "Godawful crappy time for this to come up. Some dumb hippie probably picked my pocket, who knows? There's not anything I can tell the sheriff about it."

"You don't want to be tried by *The Timberjay*," said Jack.

"Geget. I know how to talk to these people." Michael felt a small, sick fluttering below his left breast. "This will be old news by election time."

Jack nodded, his eyes on the road and his hands still and heavy on the steering wheel.

Michael affirmed to the deputy that yes, he was the

Michael Washington on the driver's license. "Do you know how his driver's license could have ended up with the body of the remains?" Michael replied that he had no idea how it had ended up with the hiker who had died in the shed.

Jack could see what Sonny was thinking: how did Michael know that the man had died in the shed? "Michael," he began, about to suggest getting in touch with a lawyer, but Michael kept talking.

"I remember that I lost a license once."

"Do you remember when that was?"

"No, just that I noticed that it was gone, when I looked for it I wasn't able to find it, and after a while when it was time to renew it, I got a new one. There's probably a record of that, right?"

The Duluth paper was the first to report that the coroner believed that the deceased man, who was possibly Native American and likely between the ages of sixteen and thirty, had died of causes undetermined. Mozhay Point law enforcement had no record of a man reported missing from the area a half-century ago that anyone could remember. An anonymous source had told the reporter that the only injury that the medical examiner could verify was a hairline skull fracture; the hiker might have hit his head and lay down to sleep in the abandoned shed on the old Odanang settlement, where he had died. The reporter provided a telephone number that anyone who had a tip could call, along with a statement from the county sheriff that the investigation would continue.

Within a month, the media lost interest, but not the people of Mozhay Point.

*

As seasons changed, autumn to winter, Michael, or sometimes Merrilee and Ann, drove Theresa to her medical
appointments. Some were twice a week and some every
day, some in Mesabi and some in Duluth. Theresa's hair
continued to thin; she bought a wig that she wore once,
decided it felt hot and looked wiffy, and then made an
appointment at a salon in Virginia to have her own hair
bobbed and feathered.

"This style is adorable on you," said the hair stylist.
"Really shows off that pretty color, almost like a pale peri-
winkle, and with your big brown eyes you look like a flap-
per!" He told her that the cut was complimentary because
she was a new customer. Theresa asked for his help in picking out some barrettes and a headband, hoping that he
would receive some commission, and left him a tip equal to
the price of the cut.

In the bathroom at home, she held a hand to view her
bobbed hair from the side and back. She shook her head;
the curving ends of the bob swung and bounced.

Margie crocheted a hat for Theresa—uneven and lumpy,
but in Theresa's favorite shade of lilac. While Merrilee sat
with her mother during her semiweekly infusion at the
cancer clinic in Duluth, Ann bought a silk flower at Hobby
Lobby in the same shade of lilac that she tacked over the gap
on the side of the hat where Margie had missed picking up
a crochet stitch.

Theresa put the hat on before she left with Merrilee
and Ann for her next appointment at the oncologist's
office. As she settled in the passenger side seat, the unseen
minidmooyenhag—Therese LaForce in the rear passenger side seat and Artense, Maggie, Beryl, and Grace in the
hatchback—nodded approvingly.

"Theresa can really wear a hat, can't she?" asked Maggie. "The color is so pretty on her, too."

"Yes, the color really suits her," answered Therese. "And that big flower over on the side really shows off her perfect features."

Artense, fighting nausea from the car ride, swallowed and took a deep breath.

"Margie is a better crocheter than I expected," commented Grace. "You can hardly see the lumps, and that girl with the sparkling eyes—what is her name, Ann?—pinned that flower right over those missed stitches so you can't tell. Unless you look close."

"I wish that Ann would stop fidgeting and digging around in her backpack," Artense complained. "Just settle down, would you?" She swallowed, fighting down a wave of nausea. "Crikey, it's warm in here. That Merrilee's driving is making me seasick," she said aloud. "Maybe Therese and I could change places on the way back to Sweetgrass; what do you think?"

"Therese is the smallest, so she will need to stay where she is." Maggie spoke in her authority as second-oldest mindimooyenh. "Ann is a little restless today; she needs room to move around."

"Well, I hope they stop at a restroom soon so that we can get out for a little air." Artense fanned her face with her broad hand, wishing for a soda cracker and a Dramamine.

"Oh, found a Tic-Tac on the bottom of my backpack!" said Ann happily. "Sorry, only one—can't share." Eyes closed, she placed the mint onto her tongue prayerfully, as if it were a communion host.

"Anybody want to stop at the Holiday in about ten minutes for the bathrooms?" asked Merrilee. "Mom? Are you awake?"

Ann laid a hand lightly on Theresa's shoulder.

"Hmm? Wegonen?" Theresa had been looking unsee-ingly at the blur of scrub at the side of the highway. "Oh, sure . . . You want coffee? A Coke? I'll buy."

"In about ten minutes," Merrilee answered, "and I want to buy." She smiled at Ann in the rearview mirror. Ann smiled back nervously.

At the infusion center the nurses admired the flower on Theresa's hat, as they had admired something about her at each session—her tennis shoes, her beaded earrings, her jeans with the sequins on the back pockets. They chatted about the weather as Theresa's port was accessed. She gritted her teeth and winced, then sat back in the recliner, closing her eyes as Merrilee and Ann began the wait while chemicals coursed into her body.

In the car on the ride home, the mindimooyenyag resumed their same places, Artense coughing insistently when her mother-in-law, commenting on the comfort of the passenger side back seat, lit her clay pipe. Ann again sat in the back seat next to tiny Therese, bobbing her head up between the two front seats as she chatted with Theresa. Merrilee, unusually quiet, didn't say much until they turned onto County 5. "Ma, we've been thinking about getting married. Me and Ann."

Ann's head surfaced between the seats and turned to face Theresa. She smiled uncertainly. "We were wondering what you'd think."

Michael would come around, Theresa thought. "Me?" she said. "I think you're both . . . miraculous. Merrilee born with a caul, she's magic, and Ann, I see magic in your eyes, the way they shine. I think two miraculous people like you should be married, is what I think."

"Oh, Theresa, that's my cataract surgery—it left a reflec-tion that sparks when the light hits it sometimes—you can see that?"

"And there isn't anything magic about me," said Merrilee. "I wish there were."

"There is, there is." Theresa reached to stroke the hair of both women. "You are miraculous, both of you. I hope you can see that."

"Can we ask Fern to make one of those fancy sandwich loaves for a wedding cake?" asked Merrilee.

"I suppose they expected that Theresa had never heard of lady-lovers," said Beryl.

"Why, my own auntie lived with a woman," answered Grace.

"And after her husband died, my first husband's sister took her best friend as her wife," said Therese. "I remember her very well, so kind to the children and such a comfort to Zente."

"Every generation thinks they invented everything," sniffed Artense.

"Indeed," answered Maggie. "Debwe."

As the car passed the Adaawewigamig! Market, Ann's eye reflected the lights above the gas pumps and sparkled.

As seasons changed again, winter now to spring, Theresa's hair began to grow back, sticking up above the thinned top of her head like soft, waving antennae. And through the changes in season and Theresa's illness, through the thinning, bobbing, covering, embellishment, and reemergence of her beautiful hair and life, the deadline to file for office in the Mozhay Point 2022 tribal discussions, and the tribal council's vote on the acquisition of the LaForce allotment lands, approached.

As Jack had anticipated, speculation regarding Michael Washington's involvement in the death of the unidentified man resurfaced. "Who could the dead man be?" was asked and wondered about in the Elders' Club in the casino, at the tobacco shop in the gas station, and in the teachers' lounge at the elementary school. Where might the dead man have come from, and where was he going? The most intriguing question of all: how did Michael Washington's driver's license come to be on the corpse of an unidentified young man from decades ago? How did this happen, and what might Michael's involvement be? The story, now back in the media, grew like seeds planted in fertile soil as it intertwined with the histories of tribal dealings and relationships at Mozhay Point from a half-century ago.

Waiting in line at Adaawewigamig! to pay for her gas and a *People* magazine, Margie suddenly saw stars. "Can you—" she started to say and then collapsed into, so she thought, a mud puddle with a brilliant oil slick of rainbow colors swirling in curlicues on its brown, translucent surface. While in the emergency room she was admitted to Mesabi Hospital for further observation. The testing, she was told, would take three days. She would miss the chance to make her presentation at the tribal council meeting.

"I can only stay a day, then I have something important I have to do back at Mozhay," she explained to the hospitalist. "I'm feeling fine. They told me I don't have a concussion." She fell asleep before she finished the sentence. When she woke, the hospitalist was gone but *Beryl Duhlebon was sitting in the chair next to her hospital bed, smoking a cigarette with a long ash about to fall onto her lucky sweater, the Mickey Mouse one with sequins.*

"Auntie," Margie said, "I'm so glad you're here. Can you tell the doctor that I have to get to the tribal council meeting?" Also, would it be impolite to tell Beryl that smoking wasn't allowed in the hospital?

Beryl looked on the bedside table for an ashtray, her lucky butterfly earrings dangling; seeing none, she flicked the ash into the palm of her hand and disappeared and Margie again fell asleep.

Later, the IHS doctor at the Mozhay clinic told Margie that she would have to stay for another day, and so she watched the council meeting on Zoom as her daughter, Crystal, read Margie's statement.

Beryl, the four puffs at the top of her updo that she called flirt curls freshly teased and sprayed, unfolded her lawn chair and sat next to her honorary niece's hospital bed to view the meeting, "Your girl did a good job; she is her mother's daughter," she said. Margie, who may have heard Beryl speak, smiled proudly.

With filings for office approaching, and the April runoff election in sight, the Tribal Executive Council tabled the vote on the planning commission's recommendation until after the June elections. By the deadline to file for office the following Tuesday, Fred Simon was the only candidate to file for the urban representative seat; his name alone would be on the ballot in June. Five people had submitted their candidacies for the at-large seat that had long been held by Michael Washington: Tammy Ricebird, blackjack dealer at Chi Waabik; Jiminy Robillard, cashier at Adaawewigamig!; Celeste LePine, Head Start teacher; Yvonne Lampi, food service supervisor at Agwaching; and Dag Bjornborg, EMT at Mozhay Point Rescue.

At 3:30, a half-hour before closing, Michael Washington paid his five-dollar filing fee and filled out his resubmission for candidacy. After an April runoff, two of the six would move forward to the June ballot.

*

Michael Washington had some private thoughts about his candidacy and the recent developments in the community:

My wife, Theresa, and I have a lot of secrets from each other. One more won't make any difference. I think there is a real possibility that Margie might have taken my driver's license—why, I don't know; she probably wanted a souvenir, a piece of me. And now her silly neediness could hinky the election, and the recreation center, the connecting road, and financial future of Mozhay Point. How that hippie's driver's license got from Margie to the body in the shed I don't know, but I would bet good money that she does.

What does Theresa know, I wonder?

I met Theresa in Duluth, at the college there where I went for a couple of days, and I met Margie because she was a friend of Theresa's. She has this way of twining herself around people, Margie. A clinging vine, is what I would call her, hard to get rid of, but then that is partly my own fault.

Theresa walked into a class and sat at the other end of the back row where I was sitting, the only other Indian I saw there. She started talking to me after class, and we got along just like that: she invited me to the room she was renting and made us supper on a hot plate. Watching her standing there mixing rice and tuna and mushroom soup, her hair and her hips swinging back and forth as she stirred, I felt like she was working some jiibik on me. When she added the can of peas, mixing them in careful so as to not break them, I was sure of it.

Before I left—that place, UMD, was not for me—I gave her a couple of phone numbers where she could call me and invited her to come up to Mozhay Point to visit sometime. She drove up a few months later, in winter, and brought her friend Margie with. The girls picked me up at Tuomela's gas station, at the Dionne Fork, and that was the first time I saw Margie, that day we went out to check my snares for rabbit, and me and my dad cooked stew while Theresa made frybread. Margie was one of those nervous types that can get on my nerves; she got a little chatty that day, talked too much, but my dad was kind to her. That's his way.

Theresa and me, we were in touch, but she didn't want to miss school, and we didn't see each other in person again until the Mozhay spring powwow, again with Margie, who didn't have much to say that time. They were a couple of eye-catching girls, stepping so careful because they were wearing these clogs with thick soles; the chainette fringe at the bottom hung in a perfect, even line that swayed as they danced. I will admit here that I was showing off, dancing and whirling in front of them.

The next summer, I got a job taking care of repairs and cleaning at Sonfish Bible Camp, on Sunfish Lake just outside of Mesabi, and took a room in town. Theresa was living with her mother at the air base housing in Duluth and had a summer job she liked at the college, filing records in some basement room where she said it was nice and cool. She drove up to Virginia and stayed with me sometimes.

What happened with my driver's license—and I have thought this over many times and this just makes sense—got started when my dad, Zho Wash, decided at the end of that summer that he was getting too old and wasn't going to rice anymore. There was a good rice crop that year, not the best time to lose your ricing partner. Zho Wash thought of Margie: he had known her dad and thought that Margie had riced with her dad at Fond du Lac, outside Duluth. So I got a hold of her, and she took the bus to the Dionne Fork and got a ride to her Aunt Beryl's next door to our place, where she stayed overnight. The next morning Zho Wash drove us in his truck, with the boat, duckbill, knockers, and some gunnysacks to the boat landing on Lost Lake.

Even though we hadn't riced together before, it went all right. I poled and Margie knocked; she had a pretty good rhythm and we were getting a lot of rice in the boat. Then after a while I could tell she was getting tired, so we took a break. And that's where things took the wrong direction. I lit a cigarette, and she wanted a puff, and the next thing I knew she had leaned in close and was touching my face, stroking my mouth, her own face small and sweet under the raggy brim of Zho Wash's ricing hat that he had told her to wear to keep out the sun. She kissed me, or I kissed her, and I remembered Theresa and leaned back, away from her closed eyes and sweet lips.

"I love you," she said.

How was I supposed to answer that? I didn't.

She sat there a minute looking down at the rice on the floor of the boat. Then she picked up the rice knockers, her hands curved over the smoothness that Zho Wash had worked into the cedar over years of use. "Think we've got enough rice?" she asked in a choked voice. "Or do you want to rice some more?"

"Let's go get this weighed," I answered, "see what we've got."

She kept Zho's ricing hat yanked down around the sides of her face as I poled us back to the landing, her shoulders hunched. When the water got to knee-deep I told her to stay in the boat and got out of the boat to pull it onto the shore, close to Fred Simon's scale and truck. That would be old Fred Simon, the old man; he was the rice buyer for the co-op back then.

Zho was waiting onshore, chatting up Pearl Minogeezhik,

who seemed to be eating up the attention. "Nice out; how was it on the lake today, my boy?" he called, looking awfully spry for somebody who had gotten too old to rice.

"Oh, mino mino mino," I answered, "but I think we're done for now."

Margie handed Zho his hat, squinting in the sun. "Mmm hmm, pretty day," she mumbled. She didn't say anything more as she helped us bag the green rice into gunnysacks. Zho kept a sack for himself to do his own finishing at home, and we carried the rest to the scales next to Fred's truck. Zho wouldn't take any of the money we got from Fred, fifty cents a pound that year, so split it, then drove toward Sweetgrass, where we dropped Margie off at the end of Beryl Duhlebon's driveway.

"She's pretty quiet, Margie," Zho commented.

"Tired," I answered. "She isn't used to ricing. She probably won't go out tomorrow." I had the feeling that that wasn't the end of it.

Later that afternoon I hitchhiked to Minneapolis to stay with my mother, Lucy, for a couple of days, then did the same back to Mozhay so I wouldn't lose my job at the camp.

What I did at Sonfish Bible Camp was more than cleaning up the latrines and the cottages and the kitchen. I fixed broken screens and beds that the Sonfishers had jumped on, cleared and sorted out the crafts, did chores for the cook— a lot of hard work during the summer. I liked it there most of the time, and I got to eat for free.

Unlike the counselors, I got to leave at the end of the day, except for the last night of each camping week, and that was the one part of the job that I didn't tell anybody about except Theresa. That part was: on that last night of camp I would drive the Sonfish van to the other side of the lake around ten o'clock, during the last campfire of the week. The camp had this outfit that I wore, a fringed suede vest and leggings, a pair of Minnetonka slippers, and a beaded headband with a zigzag design; the label said it was made in Japan. I put my hair in two braids and wore the headband over my forehead, like Tonto. All gussied up, I rowed a boat from that other side of the lake to camp and got out at the dock below the campfire. Then I walked up to the campers and talked about nature, memorized from a script that the camp director had given me. After I was done I folded my arms across my chest, told the campers to be good scouts, and rowed away. Theresa went with me a couple of times and waited in the van; she got a big kick out of the whole thing. And I'll tell you something funny: although the kids saw me cleaning up and nailing things back together every day before the campfire, not one of them ever recognized me when I was wearing that outfit.

After camp season closed in mid-August, Sonfish remained open for another month or so for adult camping sessions. I stayed on to help as long as the place stayed open, not as many hours as when the kids were there, but there would be a full week of pay, cleaning and closing up after everything was finished. The adult campers were mostly church groups who came up for a two- to three-day session, staying over one or two nights. I did my same visits, rowing from the other side of the lake, the Indian in the Boat. And it was on one of these adult campfire days, before I went into work, that I think Margie could have taken my driver's license.

It was not long after ricing season was done that I had driven Theresa's car to Zho Wash's to pick up some wild rice for Sonfish to sell to the adult campers in half-pound bags in the gift shop. This was a good arrangement for everybody.

The campers got to buy some real genuine authentic Indian wild rice, hand-finished by real authentic genuine Indians, a great addition to their souvenir Sonfish Bible Camp sweatshirts and key chains. And Zho and me got a better price than selling at Tuomelas' or to the SuperValu in Mesabi.

Zho's truck wasn't in the yard when I arrived, and it didn't look like there was anybody at the house. I opened the back door and looked into the kitchen and front room, which looked different from the way it usually did, all cleaned up, nothing lying around on the floor, Zho's coffee cups—he had a couple dozen that he'd got as gifts or at rummage sales—missing from where they usually cluttered up the kitchen table and counter.

"Hmm," I thought and went into the bedroom, which is where we kept the rice because it was dry there. I took out my wallet and set it on the little table by the bed, by the pictures of Zho's first wife, Eva, and my mother, Lucy, so that I would remember to leave some money for the rice. I was about to open one of the sacks when Margie, who must have been in the outhouse, walked in the back door.

"Oh!" she said, her mouth a little circle like a Cheerio.

"Zho Wash home? I came to get some rice."

"Noooo . . . Do you want any help?"

"I've got it, Margie, but thanks."

She sat on the bed while I scooped the rice into the bag I'd brought. I could feel her eyes round and brown on my back and hurried up. I set the bag on the bed while I tied up the top of the sack of rice in the corner of the bedroom, and when I turned around she was right there, just a few inches away. I felt as though she was sucking in the air around me, like she would never let it out.

"Michael," she said and put her arms around me. I took a

step away from her toward the bag of rice on the bed. Tripping over the rag rug on the floor, I sat on the edge of the bed, and Margie moved to between my knees.

"Michael," she said again and bent to kiss me. She tasted sweet, as she had when we stopped for that break while we were ricing, and just as I had then, I kissed her back. But this time things were different: she wrapped her arms around my neck and crossed them, I wrapped mine around her waist and rested them on her hips. She was so small, softer and more curvy than Theresa—and it was then, remembering Theresa, that I froze. Margie kept on kissing me, moving her mouth as though she was eating; I felt like she was going to start chewing, and that there might be other ways for Windigo to devour a person than the shaking of ground and the ripping of flesh. The hair on my arms and legs stood up; I pulled Margie's arms from around my neck and stood up as well. Then I picked up the bag of rice from the bed and walked out of the bedroom, through the front room, and out the door to the Nova.

I opened the back door and put the bag of rice on the back seat, got into the driver's seat, and reached in my pocket for the keys.

They weren't there. There was no way I was going back inside the house. I sat on the front steps instead to figure out how I could get the keys to Theresa's car. Thinking back on it now, Margie could have taken my driver's license out of my wallet and kept it, a piece of me that she could carry with her, like a spell she was getting ready to cast. When the time came, she would be ready.

It was always about Sweetgrass—for Zho Wash and the Muskrat family that become the Washingtons and lost the land, and for Margie and the LaForces who received the land as their allotment—and it still is.

ishpiming (heaven)

THOSE MUGS THAT YOU CAN BUY in the gift shop at Chi Waabik—the ones that every elder got for Christmas last year, along with a ham and a gift card—say it in plain words, in a circle around the Mozhay Point Band of Chippewa logo: WORLD'S BEST WILD RICE AND MAPLE SYRUP. Debwe, it's the truth: the mugs don't lie.

During my lifetime a lot has changed at Mozhay: the casino grew from a row of slot machines in Dewey Ricebird's garage to the gaming operation it is now, with the restaurant and gift shop, the cultural center and golf course. The elementary school, the one that replaced the first one that shared space with the bingo hall, was designed by a Native architect and is a real showplace; the tribal buildings include a fitness center and an arena big enough for powwows when the weather doesn't hold. Through all that, though, the old-time traditions and ceremonies have stayed with us. I'd say that tradition has made the changes, the ones that are good ones, possible.

People still go ricing and maple sugaring, both of them tied into those traditions and ceremonies, and both a lot of hard work and a lot of fun. They mean a lot, and I remember how people have done these things for a long time. I love the wild rice harvest, that short couple of weeks at the end of summer, and I love the maple sugar harvest in early spring even more. And I can say without any doubt that not only is Mozhay wild rice and maple sugar the world's best but that the maple syrup, and the sugar and candy, that come from the sugar bush at Sweetgrass is probably the best in Mozhay Point. The LaForce family, and before them the Muskrats who were renamed the Washingtons by the Indian agent at the time, have taken good care of their sugar bush, those stands of sugar maples and some birches, too, for generations.

I'm not from the LaForce or Muskrat families and can't speak for them, but for myself, Eugene Dionne, I wouldn't want to see Sweetgrass bought and taken over by anybody else, including the tribal government. It would be a cruel thing to do to those families, and to Margie Gallette, who brought those families back together when her daughter, Crystal, was born. And as Ojibwe people we have been taught by our elders, who were taught by their elders, to be thankful, humble, generous, and considerate of our families and the world around us. It goes without saying that we should try not to cause harm, even unintentionally. And it is that idea, of what is intentional and what is unintentional, that I think about often these days.

It was half a century ago, but I remember a lot about that summer so clearly, of course. I'd been going to ask a friend of mine, Punkin Minogeezhik, to borrow his driver's license for a day. The kind of person Punkin was, he would give you anything, even if you didn't ask for it; he was very traditional in that way. Punkin wasn't what people call book-smart but he was smart in other ways: he could do card tricks, for one thing, and he had a real feel for carburetors. He hadn't finished school, and the Army didn't take him because of his heart murmur; he lived with his grandfather taking care of the old man and helping people out, sometimes for pay but never expecting it, and he did some work in Tuomelas' garage with me. When the Tuomelas retired and Mozhay Point bought the store and gas station, Punkin was the first person they hired to work in the garage. He stayed there until his heart attack. But I'm getting ahead of myself.

I worked for the Tuomelas, mostly in their garage, and also delivering mail, and Dale Ann worked there part-time when she was still in school. The Tuomelas really liked her, and they hired her back when she came back from living in Chicago, and when she came back the second time after she had left the convent in Duluth where she had gone to be a nun. Our fathers were cousins, and we were friends.

After leaving Mozhay and coming back, she was really a changed person. I knew she had her troubles that she never talked about. One day she told me about this girl who was her roommate when she lived in Chicago, that the girl needed a favor, and since it was Dale Ann, I told her I would help bring a friend of the girl into Canada. He was going to pay Dale Ann some money, but I figured that Dale Ann must have other reasons than the money, and because it was Dale Ann I said I would do it, drive him to Canada and get him an ID so we could get past the border patrol at the crossing.

I thought of Punkin first because he was the kind of person who would do the same for me, no questions asked. But as it happened I never asked him.

A few days before we were going to pick up the guy from the bus stop in Mesabi, I still hadn't got around to talking with Punkin yet about his license and planned to that day after work. There wasn't much mail to deliver to the houses along the road to Sweetgrass that day except for Beryl Duhlebon, who liked catalogs and got a lot of them in her fancy pink mailbox. Zho Wash's mailbox, next on the route, was missing from the sawhorse he had tied it to—not the first time—so to deliver his mail I drove up the driveway that was always so overgrown you couldn't see anything from the road. When I pulled up to the house, Zho's old blue Ford wasn't there, but a white Nova, a fairly new car, was parked there. Michael Washington was sitting on the front stairs.

"Boozhoo. That's a nice car," I said. I knew it was his girl-friend Theresa's and that she visited him a lot in Mesabi. "Is your dad around?"

"I don't know where he is," Michael answered. He looked, as Mrs. Tuomela would say, as wrung out as an old dishcloth. "I heard he went to Minneapolis to see my mom; she's been sick."

Everybody in Mozhay knew that Lucy Washington was alcoholic and had troubles with her health. "Geez, sorry to hear that. Will he be bringing her back here?"

"No. She sees the doctor at the IHS clinic or in the emergency room when she needs to down there, and she likes it near the Round-Up, says that's her bar, there on Franklin Avenue. Anyway, says she won't leave her friends there. Eugene, would you do me a favor and go inside the house and get my car keys? They're on the kitchen table."

"Sure, Niij." I wondered what the heck was going on.

I went inside the front door, and standing there was that girl I had heard was staying at Zho Wash's house with no place to go, her eyes big and round, and her mouth formed into this little *o* like she was surprised to see me. At first I thought I startled her, that she wasn't used to people walking in without knocking or ringing a doorbell, the way they did at Mozhay in those days. She looked about fifteen years old, just a little girl, and she looked . . . *guilty* is the word that came to mind. Peachy-pink-faced and jumpy as a finch, she introduced herself.

"I'm Margie," she said all short of breath, her eyes moving nervously from the floor to the door, from the new-looking scatter rug on the front room floor to the kitchen table, from the front room window to the bedroom doorway, where I saw right away a wallet with an eagle painted on the front lying on the floor just under the bed frame. Margie's eyes went to the same place. She smiled sickly.

Trouble is what I thought.

"Eugene," I said. "I'm a friend of Michael's. He asked me to bring him his keys."

"Oh, sure, I'll get them!" She quivered into the kitchen, a wreck.

"I see his wallet; I'll get it," I said and picked it up from the bedroom floor. It was open, everything in it half-falling out onto the floor, including his driver's license, like mine, white plastic with a design of light blue pine trees scattered across. I palmed it.

A crime of opportunity, you could say, committed without a thought. I'd just been thinking, as I drove the road to Sweetgrass delivering mail, that it wasn't very likely that the draft dodger, or whatever he was, would match up very well with Punkin's driver's license, given Punkin's size. But it worked fine with Michael's—or would have, if we had gotten to Canada.

"Here's the keys," said the jittery girl. A small toy telephone the same shade of peachy-pink as her flushed face dangled from the chain.

"It was nice meeting you, Margie," I said.

"You, too!" she chirped, now a little teary.

Outside, I handed Michael his keys and wallet. "Say hello to Theresa for me," I said and left.

The four anjeniwag settled their lawn chairs in the front room of the house at Sweetgrass: Sis next to Dale Ann, Artense next to Theresa, Beryl next to Fern Dionne, newly invited to the group, Therese LaForce next to Margie, who was enthroned in her new recliner, a gift from the Council of Elders.

"I love this bathrobe; I feel like Michelle Obama in it. Migwech, nijikwewag." Margie wiggled her feet in their fuzzy socks.

"What do you want me to get you before we start the movie?" Dale Ann asked. "You want a slice of sandwich loaf, right?"

"Yes, sandwich loaf! And a couple of those cheese puffs, and some of that guacamole on a cracker."

"That sandwich loaf looks like a wedding cake, Fern," said Theresa.

Fern blushed, pleased. "Thanks. I'm practicing for the wedding."

"Did anybody bring wine?" asked Margie.

"In honor of you still not being allowed alcohol yet, no," said Theresa. "We have apple juice."

"Oh, my, that food looks delicious," said Beryl. "And look how careful they are with those luncheon plates. And that sandwich loaf—a shame we can't eat it."

"It could be worse: Grace could have brought cookies,"
snickered Sis.

"We should ask her to come with the next time the girls get
together," said Therese LaForce. "She would like that, and to
see Margie's house with the new green paint in the kitchen."

Artense inspected the paint job for streaks and misses.
"Very neat work. The girls did this themselves?"

"Dale Ann and Fern. And that new window with the plants
in it, like a little greenhouse—it's like being outside. You can
sit at the kitchen table and see the lilac bushes Margie planted
over where the outhouse was: they sure grew fast," said Beryl.

"No wonder," commented Artense.

"What movie are we going to watch tonight?" asked Sis.

"I believe they decided on Sleepless in Seattle.*"*

"Oh, I like that one, don't you?"

"Ready, everybody?" Dale Ann asked and pressed the play
button. Margie, Dale Ann, Fern, and Theresa began to eat,
their dessert forks clinking faintly and pleasantly on Beryl's
flowered pink luncheon plates, a legacy to Margie.

opiichii nagamo
minawaa

AT NINETEEN, when Margie had found her way to the Sweet-grass cabin, at first she took no comfort in the shelter provided by both Michael's father, Zho Washington, and the shadows of the ancestors. She wept often, especially in early mornings, her sadness accompanied by the birdsongs led by the first robin of the day.

"What is there to sing about?" she asked that first robin one morning when she thought Zho Wash was still out for his morning prayers, and necessities, in the woods behind the cabin. As he came around the corner back of the wood-pile he answered.

"Opiichii, the robin? Why wouldn't he sing?"

"The robin story—it is so sad, the woman in the red apron looking for her children."

"Oh, that is a sad story, Margie-ens, that the woman lost her children. She begged the Creator to help her look all over the land, and that is how the robin came to be."

Margie nodded. "She calls for her children, but they are never found."

"Yes, a very sad story. But there's more than one story about the robin." Zho sat next to Margie on the soft, yielding wooden step. "See up there, how Opiichii is at the top of the tree, leading all the other birds, and how their songs go back and forth in the trees and over the land, right down to where we are sitting?"

Margie pictured the ribbons of song weaving in and out of the trees, creating patterns that lay over the yard outside the cabin.

"It's their job; see, after the Great Flood, when the trees and plants were growing again, and the animals and birds were going to come back, Nanaboozhoo held all the birds in his arms, and he told them they were going to be the messengers of the stories, everything that ever was, and everything that was going to be, and that Opiichii would be the first one to sing every morning, the one to get things going. And then he raised his arms, throwing them up into the air, and they flew around in the sky, and Opiichii began to sing, and they all joined in."

And although the journey to knowing would be a long one, things began, in just the smallest of ways, to make sense to Margie, at nineteen.

Minawaa, in the story that repeats and cycles in the spiral of time passing, Margie at twenty was once again up early, with the robins. Comforted by the daybreaks that changed with the seasons and repeated with the seasons—just as they had long before the Muskrat family that became known as the Washingtons lived there, before Zho Wash's great-grandmother had buried his grandfather's odisimaa bag filled with sweetgrass surrounding his umbilical cord, and long before the removal of the Washingtons by the government and the assigning of the land to Margie's own great-grandfather, Half-Dime LaForce.

An hour before dawn that early fall day on the LaForce allotment land, the long fingers of the sun pushed at the edge of the dark sky, lightening the horizon and waking a robin who cautiously poked its head from the woodpile next to the Sweetgrass cabin. Swiveling his head to the right and to the left and back again, looking with first one eye and then the other for hungry predators—a fox, a hawk, perhaps even a lynx—he squeezed the rest of his body from the space where he had slept, briefly thanking the Creator that Zho Wash piled the wood he had split loosely enough for air to circulate. He perched, preened the long feathers of his wings, then flew suddenly skyward, settling on the topmost branch of the tallest aspen back of the outhouse, the most healthily nourished and with the most satisfactorily flexible branches.

"Beautiful morning," he said to himself, "and time to sing the sun up from the edge of Lost Lake."

His song, a solitary voice repeating several rounds of his wake-up song *Opi chii, opii chii niin; opiichii, nagamo daa!* was joined by other robins who woke and joined, each flying to a branch that swayed with the bird's weight and the sweetgrass-scented breeze from the swamp side of the LaForce land. Lacing phrases and melodies of their own compositions and spirits, robins were joined by cardinals, chickadees, each with its own morning song, some notes long and assertive, some more of a whistle, some a chatty warble.

The back door of the Sweetgrass cabin opened, and an old man walked slowly and deliberately toward a tamarack tree. *Zho WAASH! Zho WAASH!* sang the robin that had slept in the woodpile. At the foot of the tamarack the man stopped to look up into the branches, green and feathery. He opened a small drawstring bag that hung on a cord from his neck. From the bag he drew a generous pinch of tobacco that he placed under the tree and prayed. Then he walked past the outhouse and a short distance into the woods, considerate of the life expectancy and frailty of the outhouse and of the young woman who shared his house.

Inside the Sweetgrass cabin, Margie Robineau, a mother at twenty-one, looked into the crib to make sure that the baby was still asleep, then tied on her tennis shoes for her morning trip to the outhouse. Outside, the sky overhead grew brighter to the song of robins joined and grown louder by finches, sparrows, and grackles.

"What are they saying to each other?" she asked the morning air as she walked to the carefully maintained and used as lightly as possible outhouse. Zho Wash had told her about the times, long ago, when animals, birds, and people could talk to each other, understand each other. Raising her face to the treetops she addressed the question to the birds. "Wegonen gidikidoowin, wegonen ginaagamoowin?" she called as musically as she could.

Unlatching the door, she took a deep breath that she held as long as she could and expelled as slowly as she could. After months of practice, on any morning she was able to not inhale at all while inside. Would this morning be one? she wondered, which nearly threw off her timing, but not quite. Latching the door closed she inhaled as deeply and appreciatively as did Zho Wash as he began his prayers.

Back inside the cabin, Zho Wash was holding Crystal, wrapped in the shawl Beryl Duhlebon had crocheted in a brilliant zigzag pattern of rose and coral that dazzled the eye. He was singing the song about the bright and clear sky, his soft voice a soothing rumble. "There's coffee made," he said.

"I think I'll feed her first; she must be ready to eat," Margie said.

"Baby-ens bakade, ina?" Zho asked and handed Crystal to her mother, who smiled lovingly. In return, Crystal frowned ferociously; her face reddened, her eyes crossed and focused on Margie's forehead, and she filled her diaper loudly and mightily.

"What in the heck!" Zho laughed.

"Maybe it's the blanket; it's her way of telling us what she thinks of it," Margie answered.

"I can change her; you drink your coffee."

Who wouldn't love this man? "I'll fix a cup for you, too, and we can drink it on the front stairs," Margie said. Outside, she listened again to the birds, turning her head from one side to the other, as the first robin of the morning had done, but didn't understand the song. "OPII-chii, OPII-chi," she sang softly to herself. She sipped her coffee and called into the house, "Zho Wash, you know how people and birds used to be able to talk to each other a long time ago? Do you think that will ever happen again?" she had asked.

"Who knows, Margie-ens? Maybe sometime we'll find that out."

This morning, Margie at seventy woke early, as she had for the past half-century, her sleeping self as always aware of the coming dawn, and listened for the first robin of the day. She rose easily, the dizziness of the past several days gone, and walked out into the front room, where Theresa slept under the quilt that Joey used when he slept at the cabin, snoring a light, even buzz.

"Theresa." Margie stroked her friend's soft silver hair. Theresa turned slightly, pulled the quilt around her ear, and sighed in her sleep. From the edge of the quilt her thin braid trailed nearly to the floor.

Margie thought she saw movement out in the yard, through the window of the enclosed front porch, built over the stairs she sat on with Zho Wash when he had told her about the robins. Or was it the rocking chair in the corner next to the window rocking by itself? Margie blinked, her eyes dazzled by the rose and coral crochet pattern of the baby shawl hung over the back, Crystal's baby shawl. "Goodness, those zigzags make the chair look like it's rocking by itself," she thought. Feeling the dizziness return she sat in the chair, turned her head to rest her face against the shawl, and rocked slowly for a minute.

When Margie opened her eyes again she could see them, a group of old women seated in the yard in front of the front porch in a semicircle of webbed lawn chairs, drinking from coffee cups and chatting. The woman in a sequined Mickey Mouse sweatshirt waved to Margie, then patted the curls in the front of her elaborate updo.

"Auntie Beryl." Margie opened the front door and stepped outside and down the steps to the grassy yard. "I bet you haven't had one of these in a long time." Grace Dionne held out a Tupperware container of what looked like chocolate chip cookies. Beryl's longtime best friend, Sis, unfolded a lawn chair with flourish. "Namadabin!" she said, and Margie sat down.

A robin squeezed out from a small space between split logs in the woodpile, swiveled his head, and preened, then flew to the top branch of the tallest aspen and began to sing, the first note of the day.

Margie, the ladies, and the birds of Mozhay Point joined in, all understanding each others' songs.

LINDA LEGARDE GROVER is professor emerita of American Indian studies at the University of Minnesota, Duluth and a member of the Bois Forte Band of Ojibwe. Her novels *The Road Back to Sweetgrass* and *In the Night of Memory*, published by the University of Minnesota Press, also tell stories and histories of Mozhay Point and the Gallette, LaForce, and Washington families. She has also written *Onigamiising: Seasons of an Ojibwe Year* and *Gichigami Hearts: Stories and Histories from Misaabekong*, as well as *The Sky Watched: Poems of Ojibwe Lives.* Her fiction collection *The Dance Boots* received the Flannery O'Connor Award for Short Fiction and the Janet Heidinger Kafka Prize.